"You need to

"Is that an order, Captain?"

"A strong suggestion."

"And if I don't comply?"

"Then I will help you to do that." Trey's eyes glittered in the darkness.

"You're not army anymore."

"No, ma'am. Just a carpenter, but I will see you to the exit, one way or another."

"If I don't cooperate, what do you intend to do about it?" Sage fired off the challenge, her gut tightening at the look that rose in his face.

He stood, feet slightly apart, hands loose at his sides. "Sage, you need to leave this theater for your own safety. If I have to carry you out kicking and screaming, I am prepared for that contingency."

She heard the hardened resolution in his voice. Dimples and charming drawl aside, she knew he would not hesitate, and she was no match for his size and strength. She would lose this battle.

But not the war.

Books by Dana Mentink

Love Inspired Suspense

Killer Cargo
Flashover
Race to Rescue
Endless Night
Betrayal in the Badlands
Turbulence
Buried Truth
Escape from the Badlands
*Lost Legacy
*Dangerous Melody
*Final Resort
†Shock Wave

*Treasure Seekers
†Stormswept

DANA MENTINK

lives in California, where the weather is golden and the cheese is divine. Her family includes two girls (affectionately nicknamed Yogi and Boo Boo). Papa Bear works for the fire department; he met Dana doing a dinner theater production of *The Velveteen Rabbit*. Ironically, their parts were husband and wife.

Dana is a 2009 American Christian Fiction Writers Book of the Year finalist for romantic suspense and an award winner in the Pacific Northwest Writers Literary Contest. Her novel *Betrayal in the Badlands* won a 2010 *RT Book Reviews* Reviewers' Choice Award. She has enjoyed writing a mystery series for Barbour Books and more than ten novels to date for the Love Inspired Suspense line.

She spent her college years competing in speech and debate tournaments all around the country. Besides writing, she busies herself teaching elementary school and reviewing books for her blog. Mostly, she loves to be home with her family, including a dog with social-anxiety problems, a chubby box turtle and a quirky parakeet.

Dana loves to hear from her readers via her website at www.danamentink.com.

SHOCK WAVE
DANA MENTINK

HARLEQUIN® LOVE INSPIRED® SUSPENSE

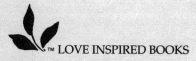 ™ LOVE INSPIRED BOOKS

ISBN-13: 978-0-373-67570-8

SHOCK WAVE

Copyright © 2013 by Dana Mentink

This edition published by arrangement with Love Inspired Books.

® and TM are trademarks of Love Inspired Books, used under license.
Trademarks indicated with ® are registered in the United States Patent
and Trademark Office, the Canadian Trade Marks Office and in other
countries.

www.LoveInspiredBooks.com

Printed in U.S.A.

The Lord is King. Let the nations tremble!
He sits on this throne between the cherubim.
Let the whole earth quake!
—*Psalms* 99:1

To those emergency workers worldwide who are the hands and feet of God in times of disaster.

ONE

The floor lurched under Trey Black's feet. Wooden planks, crippled by age and neglect, groaned like arthritic joints forced into movement. He waited one second, two.

Another quick jolt and the old Imperial Opera House stilled again.

The second jerk took him momentarily back to another place, to Afghanistan, to the smell of sun-scorched earth and gun oil, sweat and the tangible scent of fear.

He stood motionless between a row of chairs looking toward the stage, eyes scanning the ghostly fly tower with its combination of counterweights and pulleys, the rusty overhead lighting, the dusty floorboards, worn and marred. It hadn't been his imagination—a few of the fly tower ropes still quivered from the sudden movement.

His mind knew he was not in Afghanistan anymore, but his body had not learned the lesson. He rubbed the back of his neck and ran a palm over his hair, the wild thatch of it still an odd contrast to the buzz cut he'd had until he'd left the army behind a month ago.

It was not enemy fire.

Not the impact from a mortar volley.

The truth materialized.

Earthquake.

Small, probably not more than a 2.5, one of a number of quakes that had rumbled through the city in the past twenty-four hours. He'd heard some scientist on a morning talk show explaining that the miniquakes were the earth's way of releasing tension gradually as the tectonic plates ground together. Yet another scientist suggested the shakers could be warnings that the "big one" was coming.

Earthquakes were like people, he figured. Sometimes you couldn't tell if they were friendlies or enemies until it was too late. He shook away the thoughts and called softly into the darkness.

"Wally?" His voice echoed, bouncing in and out of the dark stalls, the mazelike warren of dressing rooms, rehearsal areas and the cavernous empty stage. It was a terrible place for a dog, but Trey had agreed to come check on the little critter when he was done for the evening as a favor to the caretaker. "Wally?" he said again, louder.

He caught the faintest sound, the barest squeak of a floorboard from the royal box, the ornate enclosure at the middle of the lowest tier of seating and the spot with the best sight lines to the stage. Long ago it would have been the place reserved for royalty or VIPs out for a night at the Imperial. Now, on a Sunday night, decades after the theater offered up its last real opera, it was tomblike.

He listened, body taut. The sound didn't come from the rascally dog. He wasn't sure how he knew, but he did.

Nor did he understand why he took cover behind the proscenium and began a surreptitious creep toward the noise.

No reason to suspect it was anything dangerous.

This was San Francisco, not a war zone, and he was in an empty opera house. More likely his unease was paranoia borne of long months dodging sniper bullets or worrying that a careless moment on his part would result in death.

Like the journalist embedded with their unit.

The memory bit at him before he could steel his mind against it.

He recalled the look on Sage Harrington's face when she saw her colleague hit by sniper fire. Her camera fell to the ground and those eyes, those ice-blue eyes, locked on his, soldering the two of them together in her white-hot grief. She blamed him, it was clearly written on her face.

Blamed him, when they never should have been there in the first place. He felt the burn of anger at Sage for her reckless behavior, and himself, for the stubborn way his heart still kicked up at the thought of her.

Snap out of it, Trey. Sage has to live with her decisions and you've got to live with yours.

His mind circled the facts again.

Empty opera house, closed to the public for decades.

Whoever it was making the noise was a trespasser.

Find Wally.

Get out of the Imperial and go home.

He shouldered his backpack, heavy with the tools he'd been using to try to repair and replace the rotting wood of the lobby floor. A whisper echoed over to him, a hushed voice belonging to someone who shouldn't be there. A vagrant maybe, who had forced their way through the boarded-up windows perhaps, looking to escape the clinging October chill. He could still call it quits, look for Wally on his way out. It wasn't his problem. Not his responsibility. No reason to feel like he had to protect Mr. Long's investment from intruders. No reason to stay.

He took a deep breath and crept farther into the darkness, heading for the stairs that would take him to the royal box.

The chilled air of the opera house made Sage Harrington's skin prickle all over. Her own hands looked pale and ghostly in the meager light from her lantern, shaking slightly from the temblor she'd just felt and the oppressive blackness. It was ridiculous, really. Stupid certainly, to follow Antonia inside. Not the first time she'd behaved stupidly.

Something about Antonia Verde pricked Sage's instincts. The woman knew the truth about Sage's cousin Barbara, she was sure, something Barbara's husband, Derick, wasn't telling. Then again the whole situation might just be the product of Sage's overactive imagination. Barbara might very well be in Santa Fe like her husband claimed.

In Santa Fe.

Not answering the phone.

Not returning emails.

Nearly at full-term for her pregnancy.

Without sending so much as a postcard to check on the renovations to her beloved opera house. Sage had seen Antonia do something inexplicable—pick up a picture of Barbara from the glass side table and hide it under her shirt before sneaking out of the Longs' house.

The cold feeling deep in her stomach returned. Something had happened to Barbara, and Antonia had some information that would help Sage find the truth. She'd grudgingly agreed to meet Sage at the Imperial and talk. Why in the world had they agreed to meet here?

Toughen up, Sage. She would complete her mission, as a man from her past would say, and she found she could not hold back the feelings.

How many times had she thought about Trey Black? Wondered how things would have been different if they'd gotten to know each other somewhere else instead of the hills of northeastern Afghanistan? It seemed surreal, now, that only a year ago she was snapping pictures for a top-selling news magazine, simultaneously afraid for her life and struggling against a powerful attraction toward the captain.

She flashed back to Luis, his body falling at her feet, gone, at Trey's horrified eyes in his dust-stained face. Trey's shock remained only for the barest of moments. Then he was the hardened soldier again, barking orders, shouting into a radio, his attention turned back to the task, the mission, while the medic tried frantically to save Luis's life. Trey Black, a living reminder of the worst moment in her life, simply refused to get out of her head.

Sage shook herself and tried to offer up another prayer for Barbara. No words would come. Only the same impenetrable silence, the same darkness that had cloaked her since her return.

The sound of a stair creaking stirred her senses. Though the stairs to the box were still more or less covered in tattered carpet, the old wood complained under the weight of someone's approach.

Someone? She mentally chided herself. It was

Antonia, of course, passing the time while waiting for Sage. Who else would be interested in this old relic? She wished she could shine her lantern into the stairwell, but she resisted the urge. Instead she drew back into the farthest corner of the box and held the light down behind the seat. If she'd learned anything being in a war zone it was that being cautious could save your life. Unfortunately, her caution seemed to have slid into the realm of paranoia. She'd wait to be sure it was Antonia.

A vibration started under her feet, rattling harder and harder until the building seemed to come alive around her. Earthquake—and this time, much more powerful. She held on to the arm of the seat. A rending of wood sounded above her head. It must be the overhead balcony, tearing away from its moorings.

Panic swelled through her as she fought to stand against the bucking floor.

She yanked herself upright and tried to get to the exit, but she went down on one knee again, something sharp cutting through her jeans.

A roar from above made her throw her hands over her head as a section of the ceiling gave way. Fragments of plaster and wood rained down, swallowing up her scream. Dust coated her mouth as she gasped for air, panic bringing her back to the war zone, filling her gut with black despair. There was a heavy pressure and then silence.

Sage was not sure in that moment if she was

alive or dead. Her own rasping breath confirmed that she was indeed living and conscious. Though the box was bathed in darkness, a weak light came from the gaping hole in the ceiling where the balcony above had come crashing through. A thick layer of dust drifted downward.

Just breathe, take it slow.

She coughed out a mouthful of plaster dust and took stock. Aside from general aches, she did not feel any lancing pain. Gingerly, she wiggled her legs and arms, turning her neck slowly to one side. She struggled to sit up but something heavy lay across her shoulders, pressing her down. She quelled the panic.

A few more deep breaths and she worked again on wriggling her legs, propelling herself forward since she had no hope of lifting the thick beam. Fortunately, it had fallen across the span of two seats, leaving a small spot of clearance. Sage scooted forward again, her feet scrabbling for purchase.

Maybe it was a whisper of movement, or the slow exhalation of breath, but in a sudden wash of fear, Sage knew she was not alone.

"Antonia?" she whispered.

No one answered. Perhaps she had imagined the presence. Her doctor would say it was a symptom of post-traumatic stress disorder. She caught sight of the lantern, which had tumbled down the aisle and now lay a few feet away.

She pulled herself forward, her efforts only netting her a few inches before she had to stop for breath, face bathed in a combination of sweat and grime.

The sound of quietly placed footsteps caused her to freeze. They were made by someone heavy and solid, not by the willowy Antonia.

"Who is it?" she hissed. Whoever it was came closer, but try as she might, she could not twist herself into a position to look up. Some part of her, the deep-down place where instinct lay, told her whoever was in that box had not come to help.

"People know I'm here," she said quickly. "People are coming."

The feet moved closer. Sage could feel the boards shifting and bending under the stranger's weight.

She could see only the shadow in her peripheral vision, someone watching, thinking. The gloom that settled over her pressed fear deep into her pores. She was immobilized, trapped and in darkness as this person closed the gap between them.

Her blood pounded in her veins. She would yell, but who would hear her?

In a scrabble of noise, something hurtled into the box, knocking over the lantern.

She screamed as the thing streaked at her, eyes glowing.

Then a wet tongue swabbed her face. She batted at the creature, which her brain finally identified as a dog. The exuberant tongue was attached to a wiry animal with a head that seemed too small for its lanky body.

Shoving him away, she tried to get a glimpse of the stranger.

She realized she was alone again. Whoever had left her trapped there was gone.

Relief made her shiver, and she reached out to finger the dog's velvety ears, which started out erect and then flopped over at the tips.

"Where did you come from?" she managed. He licked her again and sniffed her hair. The dog stopped midsniff, cocked his small wedge of a head.

"Hear something, boy?" she whispered, skin prickling. Was the stranger coming back?

After another moment of listening, the dog took off through the doorway.

She wanted to call after him, to bring the friendly, warm animal back. Instead she applied every ounce of her strength into freeing herself from her entrapment. Inch by painful inch she yanked herself out, scraping her legs in the process. Anger rippled through her like a shock wave. The stranger hadn't gotten far and Sage was going to find out who it was.

She heard the rumble as she ran, the faraway sound of a door being slammed, or a heavy box being dropped onto a cement floor. She reached the bottom stairs and collided with a man heading up. He was big, over six feet and solidly muscled, and her five-foot-four-inch frame bounced off his chest like a tennis ball hitting a racket.

The man's flashlight tumbled down and landed at his feet with a soft thunk.

He picked it up, holding it with one hand, the other hand readied in a fist in front of him as if he was expecting an attack.

Sage shielded her face from the light. "Who are you?"

There was a moment of hesitation. "You want my rank and serial number, or will the name suffice?"

Shock settled over her in a numbing blanket. She didn't need him to repeat the question. The Southern lilt of his voice, the smile she heard hidden in the words. There was no one else it could possibly be. He looked odd in civilian clothes, and the flicker of uncertainty on his face was definitely out of place.

She took the hand he offered and got to her feet, legs gone suddenly shaky. He pulled her up and close to him, one hand grasping hers tightly and the other cradling her shoulder with the gentlest of touches. For a moment she could not summon the strength to balance on her own and she pressed close, her heart swimming with a tide of memory that threatened to drown her. "Thank you."

Something in her voice must have sounded familiar enough. He lowered the light to play it across her face, and in doing so illuminated his own, the planes of his cheeks and forehead and the look of complete shock that materialized on his face. "It can't be," he whispered.

She heaved in a breath and stood up as straight as she could manage. "Do you want my rank and serial number? Or will the name suffice?"

Trey was not a man comfortable with conversation, and in that moment, words failed him utterly. He stared at Sage in disbelief. Her heart-shaped face, dusty though it was, those blue eyes, were unmistakable. He felt like turning on his heel and marching away to give himself time to think. Instead he forced out a glib remark. "Well, ma'am, this is better than the last place we met."

It was the wrong thing to say. Her expression grew distant and shuttered. He stumbled on. "Are you hurt? I heard a crash."

She waved a hand. "Part of the balcony fell. I'm not hurt. Just dirty."

"Why are you here in this old relic?"

She hesitated and he got the sense she was weighing how much of the truth to give him. "Taking pictures for my cousin Barbara. Her husband owns this theater."

Trey shook his head in disbelief. "Mr. Long hired me, but I didn't realize his wife was your cousin."

"So you haven't seen her recently?" There was something akin to hope shining in her face as she spoke the question.

"No."

The emotion seemed to drain from Sage and her shoulders slumped. He wondered what he'd said, or hadn't said.

She gave him a hard stare. "Was there… Did you see anyone else here?"

Odd question. "No one. Why?"

"I thought…" She shook her head. "Never mind. I've been watching too much TV or something. I'm sure it was just my imagination."

He looked her over and noted the latent fear circling under her calm expression. He decided on an oblique approach. "Kinda late in the day to be taking pictures."

She eyed him with that gleam of determination and shrewdness that always saw right through any smoke screen he'd ever tried to float by her. "Late for you, too. And late for the painter. Her name is Antonia, and I happen to know she's inside the Imperial now. So what's your reason for being here?"

Wally scampered up the stairs, his whip of a tail wagging in frantic rhythm. "He is. I'm a friend of the caretaker, kind of. He asked me to come by and make sure this little guy was safe and secure in the utility room. I guess I'll have to report your misconduct, Wally. You're out of your assigned area, soldier." He eyed Sage again. "Why don't you tell me who or what you're really looking for?"

She started. "What makes you think I'm looking for something?"

His lip curled. "Your straight face isn't too convincing, not to mention the fact that I don't see any camera." He thought she was going to let him have it, but she smiled that amazing grin that made something in the pit of his stomach flutter around.

"I knew I forgot something. Left my camera in the car." After a moment, her smile slowly vanished.

He was not sure what to say, how to counter the shadow that hung heavily between them. Luis was the face that swam in Trey's dreams, the civilian who had died on Trey's watch. He'd been so right to protest taking outsiders into a war zone, dead right, but he could see in her expression that she still didn't accept that, wouldn't take responsibility for her part in Luis's death. A creaking under their feet hinted that the old theater was settling again, sinking under the weight of unseen pressure.

"Isn't safe to be in here. I'll walk you out."

"I'll find Antonia first and tell her I'm leaving. She was here a few minutes ago."

"This place is a death trap. We'll go now and I'll come back and find her after you're outside."

Sage moved back a step. "I'm not going and

you can't order me to. This isn't the army, Captain Black."

He fixed her with a stare. "You didn't take orders even when you were in my platoon."

"You never wanted us there."

He felt the exasperation, the anger, bubble up again, fresh as it had been a year ago. "No, I didn't and I was right. We were there to fight. There is no room in a combat zone for civilians."

"Journalists."

"Whatever."

She shook her head. "Luis and I were there to bring attention where it most needed to be. Our stories brought the public right to the front lines, to show the world what war is really like. It was worth the inconvenience to your operation."

He spoke softly, his words floating away into the darkness. "Would Luis's widow agree with you?"

The wrong thing to say, again, though every syllable was the truth. This time she didn't even attempt an answer. She pushed past him on the stairs, Wally prancing at her heels. Trey reached out and touched her shoulder, so small in his ham of a hand. "Look, I'm sorry. This isn't the time. Fact is, I'm glad to see you, Sage." *I can't stop thinking about you.*

Good thing that thought stayed in his head where it belonged. She hadn't missed him at all, judging from the way she snatched herself out of his grasp.

"Nice of you to say. I've got a job to do here, so go ahead and see yourself out."

The old building shuddered and swayed under the grip of another earthquake. The motion sent Sage off balance and he steadied her. "You're not staying in here." This time, she would not ignore him.

"I'm not leaving this opera house without talking to Antonia."

"Every once in a while you should listen to reason," he snapped. "Since you can't seem to do that, I will have to be your personal escort."

She pulled away again and flashed him a smile. "Only if you can keep up with me, Captain," she said as the blackness closed around her.

TWO

Sage's knees were shaking, but it wasn't from an earthquake. Those mischievous eyes, the dimples carved into his cheeks, the lazy twang of his Southern accent. Trey Black could not be here in the wreck of an opera house. Worse yet, it was not possible that her stomach stirred at the sight of him, nerves jangling at the touch of his big hands.

No, no, no.

It was not right, her attraction for this man that started the moment she'd clapped eyes on him. Romance had no place in a combat zone. And it had no place now, when she wanted to forget she'd ever set foot in Afghanistan and finally had something important to focus on, something that might allow her to escape the smothering blanket of PTSD that nearly crippled her.

She could feel him, sense his big presence in the stairwell behind her, and she quickened her pace. It was a useless effort. Trey Black would not approve of her trotting off into a potentially dangerous situation by herself. A woman doesn't belong around danger, he'd told her calmly with that half-teasing tone. Part of her was flattered, the other part was infuriated. He was a chauvinist. She was every bit as capable, or at least she had been before her self-confidence had blown away in an angry chatter of bullets. Way down deep at the bottom of her fury, she had the dreaded feeling that maybe Trey Black had been right.

Afghanistan had been a nightmarish combination of unbelievable courage and silent grief. She saw it in the eyes of the soldiers when one of their comrades fell and behind their stoic expressions when things went bad. And she'd forced herself in, obtaining approval by using her connections. So where did the blame really belong?

She shook her head to clear it.

Don't go back there.

Her cell phone chimed and she answered it, still moving down the stairs.

A deep voice filled the line. "It's Derick."

That brought her up short. She could picture his fiftysomething face, still with that luminous big-screen quality and easy charm, the perfect thatch of sandy hair. "Hello. It's good to hear from you."

He blew out a breath. "I was worried. Are you all right? Just had another quake and the Imperial is a collapse waiting to happen. I was afraid you might be buried alive."

She wondered how he knew she was at the opera house. "I'm okay. A chunk of ceiling came down."

He gasped. "You must leave there immediately. It's not safe and Barbara would never forgive me if something happened to you."

She wished she could hear Barbara say those words. "I'm on my way out right now. What can I do for you?"

"I want you to reconsider staying with us here. I know Barbara wouldn't want you to be in a hotel, especially with all these quakes happening. We've got plenty of extra rooms, even with Antonia staying in the guest house."

"I'm fine, thanks."

"You've been worried about Barbara." He laughed. "You think I've stuffed her away in some closet, I gather."

"No, of course not," she said, mentally berating herself for not taking things slower with Derick. "I just worry about her, with her pregnancy and all. It didn't seem like a reasonable idea to take a trip when she's due to deliver twins in a matter of weeks."

He sighed. "Anyone who knows Barbara would agree that she is one headstrong lady. That's what I love about her. It's maddening, but we make it work for the most part."

Sage didn't know what to say about that. He sounded perfectly sincere, but he was an actor. It was his job to sound sincere. To hear him tell it, his career was in top form, but she'd heard rumblings of financial hardship, bad investments. Maybe it was just rumors. Maybe not.

"I just want you to know I received an email from her today," he continued.

Sage's heart sped up. Had she been wrong about everything? "That's great. What did she say?"

"I'll read it straight from the screen. 'So enjoying my time in Santa Fe. Tell Sage to photograph only the front lobby of the Imperial. The rest is a wreck, too dangerous. Will call soon, love and kisses, Barbara.'"

The silence stretched between them until Derick spoke again. "Sage? Did you hear that? Are you still there?"

"Yes," she managed. "I'm here. Thank you for sharing that with me. I appreciate it." Her tone sounded wooden to her own ears.

"No trouble at all. Is Antonia with you, by chance?"

Sage wasn't sure how to answer. "No," she said. "Why?"

"I need to make sure she's okay, and we have some business. If you see her, can you have her phone me?" He cleared his throat. "It's rather urgent. I've tried calling her cell, but no answer."

"Of course."

"I am on my way down to the theater to make sure everything is locked up properly."

Her stomach tightened, but she forced a light tone. "I thought you had a caretaker for that."

"I do, but Rosalind thinks more highly of him than I do. Abandoned buildings are a beacon for the homeless or kids up to no good." He chuckled. "I told Barbara the Imperial was an enormous black hole, sucking up money and attracting trouble like nobody's business. She never did see things my way."

Something about the statement chilled Sage.

"She loves the Imperial."

"Yes, she does."

"Promise me you won't go back inside."

She tried for a light tone. "I never make promises anymore."

He hesitated. "Well, at least I can be sure you don't go in there alone. I'll be along shortly. Goodbye, Sage."

Sage clicked off the phone. She hadn't realized she'd stopped moving until Trey joined her on the wide step. So Derick needed to see Antonia urgently. Not until Sage got to her first.

"Trouble?" he asked.

She nodded. "My cousin Barbara is missing."

He frowned. "How do you know that?"

"Because her husband told me she left a message directing me to photograph the front lobby only."

Trey frowned. "And?"

Sage locked eyes with Trey. "I spoke to her ten days ago. She wanted me to shoot every corner of the Imperial to document the remodeling project from the basement to the rafters. My cousin never does things halfway."

"So if the email is made up, sounds like he doesn't want you wandering around in this opera house." The concern on Trey's face deepened. "Been to the police?"

She shook her head. "I have an appointment this afternoon, but first I was going to…um, check on something."

"Sage," he started.

"Okay, okay. I just need to talk to Antonia Verde. She's the painter Derick hired. I saw her at the house and she was having a heated discussion with Derick. Very heated. They both clammed up when they saw me, but Antonia knows something. Several times I got the sense she wanted to talk to me, but she didn't want him to overhear. So we made an arrangement to meet at the theater tonight, but she got here before me. She's not answering her cell, so I figured I'd snoop around until I found her." Her cheeks warmed.

He raised an eyebrow. "Going into the detecting business? You don't seem cut out for that."

I'm not cut out for anything anymore. Sleepless nights. Panic attacks. Flashbacks and worst of all, the sense that she was dead inside. She forced her chin up. "I'm just here to talk to Antonia."

"This place…"

"I know, I know. It's not safe to stay here. I should wait outside while you go commando and find Antonia yourself, but the fact of the matter is, I'm not going to obey orders."

"Imagine my shock and disbelief." He sighed, the sound bouncing along the darkened stairwell as he picked up a pack she hadn't noticed before and handed her his flashlight.

Surprised, she took it from his calloused fingers. "You gave up easily."

"No, ma'am. I'm army and we don't give up. We just get the job done." His tone was bitter.

Sage huffed. "So you're going to shadow my every move until I leave this place?"

"That's an affirmative."

"You aren't a soldier anymore."

Her attempt to rile him didn't work. He shot her a lazy smile. "Consider me your friendly neighborhood carpenter. You never know when you might need a guy with a bag of tools."

Biting back a remark, Sage led the way down the stairwell toward the orchestra seating where the nearest exit would be. Maybe Antonia had gone right for it after the last quake, and if they didn't hurry, she'd make it outside before they caught up.

Wally pranced ahead of them and disappeared.

Suddenly she heard a shrill bark.

A figure loomed out of the darkness, and Sage screamed.

In a moment Trey was in front of her.

Heart pounding, she couldn't see around Trey's blocky shoulders until he stepped to the side to reveal an old man, bald head shining in the lantern light. Wally stood next to him, tail wagging vigorously. Even the gloom could not hide the look of irritation on the man's face.

"Whaddya doing here?" he demanded of Sage, thrusting his lantern in her direction.

Trey held up a calming hand. "Hey, Fred. Sage, this is Fred Tipley, the caretaker. Wally is his dog. I thought you were going to pack up your apartment today, Fred. Isn't that why you asked me to check in on Wally?"

"Forgot something," Fred grumbled, eyeing the dog. "I was just on my way back to my truck. Seems Wally busted out of the utility room again." The look he gave the dog pawing at his pant leg softened the edges of his face. "You're a troublemaker, Wally, sure enough," he said, giving the dog a pat. His eyes narrowed as he straightened. "Where'd you find him? Not safe to go poking around this place."

"He found me," Trey said. "No poking involved."

He pointed a gnarled finger at Sage. "What about her?"

Sage gave him a smile. "I'm working for Barbara Long. I'm her cousin, actually. She asked me to take some pictures."

"Not now, she didn't. Miss Rosalind would have called me. She manages things here, not Barbara."

Sage eyed him closely. "Barbara and her husband own this theater and I've got permission to be here."

He grumbled some more. "Dumb idea to come here in the dark. Wood's rotted. Plenty of places to hurt yourself. Didn'tcha feel that earthquake? Been happening on and off all day. Ain't you got no sense?"

Trey raised his voice a notch. "Fred, we're just finishing up here and then we're leaving for the day. I can keep Wally with me so you can go pack and I'll make sure the doors are locked when I leave, okay? Call me when you get settled into your new place and I'll bring Wally."

"Nah, never mind about that. My plans have changed. I'm here now so it's you two that need to go."

Sage bent to pet the dog that was sniffing at her shoes. "When was the last time you saw Barbara, Fred?"

He answered with a shrug. "Can't remember. While ago. Heard she was in New Mexico or something."

Right. A very pregnant woman travels to Santa Fe at a moment's notice.

"Did you ever talk to her?"

"Maybe once or twice."

"Did she hire you to work at the Imperial?"

He folded his wiry arms across his chest. "Why the third degree? I just make sure the doors stay locked and keep trespassers out."

Had he been the one who left her trapped? Sage saw from the tight set to his lips that she was not going to get any more information from him. A bead of sweat rolled down his wrinkled forehead and he swiped it away with the back of his hand. She would find out what she could about Fred Tipley and definitely mention him to the police that afternoon.

She felt Trey's gaze on her. He quirked an eyebrow. *Done with your interrogation, detective?* his eyes seemed to say.

Not anywhere close to done. Not until I find Antonia.

A metallic clank startled them all. Fred whirled in the direction of the stage. "You hear that? Someone's there."

"It's probably Antonia," Sage said, starting down the stairs again.

"What is she doin' backstage? I heard she was hired to paint the frescoes in the lobby only," Fred muttered. "Don't nobody do what they're told anymore?"

"Maybe she got disoriented in the dark," Trey

said. He tried to edge ahead of Sage but she elbowed him back.

"Now you gotta stop right there," Fred said, stepping in front of them. "Miss Rosalind said no one is to be messing around here. I could lose my job."

Trey called over his shoulder as they went around him, "Fred, I'll take care of things. We'll locate this other trespasser and I will personally escort all of us out of this place."

Fred made no attempt to follow, but his voice carried along the stairwell. "It ain't right. I'm gonna have to call Miss Rosalind. It ain't right. Wally, come here."

The dog barked and darted off again, eliciting an angry tirade from Fred.

Trey kept pace behind her and Sage felt a twinge of guilt. She called to him. "Rosalind may not take this well. I don't want to cost you your job or anything."

"A job is a job. I can get another one. I'm mostly just biding time, watching my brother's place while he's away." He paused. "How about you? Where do you call home?"

"Nowhere," she said, angry at herself for saying it out loud. "Not here, anyway. I'm just in San Francisco for Barbara."

"Kind of risking your relationship with the Longs, aren't you? Chances are you are going to be out of Derick's good graces after Fred makes his report."

She nodded. "I'm willing to take the chance. After I talk to the cops this afternoon, I don't think Mr. Long is going to ask me in for tea."

They took the rest of the steps as fast as they dared until they found themselves at tall metal doors that marked the stage entrance. Her skin prickled as she imagined the walls closing in on them, the darkness reaching out from behind to snatch them. Anxiety burgeoned in her belly like the clouds of dust that erupted under their feet. No panic attacks now. She could not stand the humiliation of turning into a helpless hysterical lump in front of Trey.

After a deep breath, Sage grabbed the handle and yanked.

"It's locked," she groaned. "Antonia must have gone to the other side. We'll have to double back."

Trey took her hand before she could leave. He pulled her closer and she felt the warmth of his body, the scent of soap on his skin. Her pulse quickened.

"Hang on, there. I think I can help with this." He fished something out of his pocket and bent over the lock, his back blocking her view. In a moment, he pushed the door open and turned to her with a cocky grin.

She gaped. "How did you do that?"

"I have skills."

She raised an eyebrow.

He shrugged and held up the key ring. "Fred gave me a spare set so I could get in and check on the dog. He forgot to take them back."

She grinned, her face unaccustomed to the expression. "So I guess you really do have skills." For a moment, things were easy between them and she wondered what it would be like if he really was just a carpenter and she just a photographer meeting for the first time. Silly thought. Too much hurt. Too much anger. Her heart was a twisted, blighted thing that would not be salved by daydreams.

His grin turned serious, swallowed up as they stepped through the double doors into the tomb-like darkness.

THREE

Trey felt a surge of cold air against his face as he eased open the door. Sage pressed against him and his breath caught. She felt just like he had imagined many times when she wasn't aggravating him, soft and warm, like a delicious breeze trickling through an Arkansas summer day. He cleared his throat and pushed through the opening. Blackness enveloped them. He groped his way to the wall while Sage held the flashlight. The small glow did little to fend off the cavernous blackness.

"Gotta be a switch around here somewhere."

"You haven't been in this part of the theater?" she whispered.

"No. Fred knows it like the back of his hand, so he showed me the places I needed to see." He found himself replying in an equally hushed voice. "Seems I was hired to repair the front lobby and that's it. Got my orders not to explore except to check on Wally."

Sage made a thoughtful sound. "That didn't seem odd to you?"

"Not really. You can see the condition of this place. Not safe for a rat. Personally, I think it's only suited to the wrecking ball."

"Barbara doesn't seem to think so. She's paying you, so the Imperial must be good for something."

He couldn't read her expression, but he caught the tone. "As I said, I get paid through Rosalind, she's the business manager, but if Barbara thinks there's value here then I stand corrected. She's smart. Figure it runs in your kin along with the stubborn streak and mouthiness."

She huffed. "And I'm sure the women in your family are all delicate flowers."

"Maybe I'll tell you about my mom sometime," he said, trying to keep the emotion out of his voice that always kicked up when he considered his mother. Sage could learn a thing or two about quiet strength from her.

"I'm beginning to agree that this place may be beyond repair," Sage said, her words swallowed up by the cavernous space.

"It's a little late for that realization," Trey said. Finally, his fingers found what he sought. He pushed up the lever and the overhead lights flicked on, at least the three that still had working bulbs.

The stage was empty in spots and crammed full in others with boxes piled into crazy stacks. Rising above the boxes was the massive wooden cutout of a clipper ship and several smaller bundles swaddled in sheets. "How did all this stuff get here?"

"The Imperial was purchased about twenty years ago by a man who sank a small fortune into mostly cosmetic repairs. They went bankrupt after only a few shows. Other people bought it, but most of the time it just sat here rotting until Barbara became involved."

Trey whistled and the sound echoed strangely. "Wonder why the Longs would want to take on such an expensive wreck? Why not demolish and rebuild?"

"Barbara's always been in love with architecture and the opera. This must have seemed like a dream opportunity for her when she married Derick and he bought it for her as a wedding gift."

Trey heard the sad lilt in her voice. "An opera house is a pretty big gift. Why would he turn around a year later and make her disappear?"

Sage locked her eyes on his. "Things can change in a year."

But some things don't, he thought. Some things last, like faith and memories…and love, at least he used to think so. A restless feeling coursed through him. The darkness pressed in on them both until he could stand the inactivity no longer. He stepped forward, but Sage grabbed his wrist. He turned, struck by the way her hair shone, a strange luminosity granted by the eerie light. "Problem?"

"I did a little studying up on the theater." She pointed to the floor. "There's a series of trapdoors built into the stage, triggered by a lever system underneath."

He squinted at the floor. "Don't see any open ones."

"Me neither, but this building has stood without any major repairs since 1919. That's a lot of time gone by for things to rust and fail."

He grinned.

"What? What's so funny?"

"Risk assessment. You sound like a platoon leader."

She shook her head. "Anyway, I don't hear Antonia."

He nodded. "Dust on the floor looks undisturbed here. Let's check back by the rear entrance in case she made her way in that direction."

Sage stepped in close behind him, her hand on his back as they crept around the perimeter toward the thick folds of curtains.

Something skittered by Sage's feet and she jumped.

"Just a rat," he said, repressing a shudder of his own. He'd die content never having to clap eyes on a rat again.

Her fingers clutched at his shirt, balling it up. A

sensation on the back of his neck made him stop and pull farther into the velvet drapery.

"What is it?" Sage whispered, her breath tickling the side of his face.

What was it? Nothing concrete, just a feeling, a sensation of eyes following his progress. He looked up at the catwalk far above them. No sign of movement, but plenty of places to conceal a watcher. What for? If it was Antonia she had no cause to climb up the catwalk and even less to stay there and spy on them. So who would be watching? And why?

He shook his head. "Nothing, I guess." The sad by-product of combat was the paranoia, the inability to fit properly into a normal world again after the shooting stopped.

Lord, help me put that behind me. Way behind.

As he scanned the shrouded shapes festooned with cobwebs and smelling of mold, he decided this was definitely not a normal situation.

As they eased toward the rear exit, his neck prickled again, the instinct that kept him alive through two tours of duty flaring to life.

Someone is watching.

Waiting.

Instinctively, he reached for the M16 that wasn't there.

He blinked hard and looked up again at the catwalk, where his eyes found nothing but shadows.

You're losing it, Black. Probably just rats up there.

As if on cue, a fist-size rodent darted along the floor a mere three feet from them.

He expected her to scream, chauvinist that he was, but she didn't. She tightened her grip on his shirt and he heard her sharp intake of breath, but she did not cry out.

She never had.

Even when the bullets started flying and one of them found the jugular artery of her friend.

When machine gun fire nearly deafened them.

When she climbed into the transport aircraft to carry Luis home for burial.

She'd never screamed.

Maybe things would be better between them if she had.

Sage steeled her spine against the shudder that rippled up and down her back. Rats. She wondered how many of them were peering at her right now from their burrows deep in the rotted walls and floor of the old place.

Her stomach quivered. She clamped her jaws shut, stuffed the fear down deep and pushed the curtain aside as they went, hoping nothing hairy would meet her searching fingers. Antonia was not hiding here, she was sure. After witnessing the poor woman nearly pass out from fright when she'd seen a mouse skitter across the front walk of the Longs' home, she knew Antonia was not likely to linger deep in these rodent-infested shadows. She must have exited through the back door.

If they made it there quickly enough, she might be able to stop Antonia from leaving until the woman came clean.

Where is my cousin?

That's all she needed to know.

Derick's words echoed through her ears.

She never did see things my way.

Derick was lying. He'd made up the email.

Another possibility struck her.

Or maybe he hadn't. Maybe Barbara had sent the email, trying to convey a message to her without alerting her husband.

Only a few yards to go before they reached the exit. Trey picked up the pace. She felt the corded muscles of his lower back tense as he moved, lithe as a tiger through the dark. Some part of her was grateful that he put enough stock in her theory to follow along.

Why was he helping? For old times' sake? Guilt about what happened to Luis? No, he was on another mission, to deliver her from a dangerous situation, just like he'd tried so hard to do in Afghanistan, like he would try to do for any hapless stranger he happened to find wandering around. He was a machine, duty above all.

Their feet stirred up puffs of dust that whirled and eddied through the stale air.

From above came the loud squeal of wood. Trey grabbed her arm so tightly she almost cried out. They looked wildly up into the darkness, trying to pinpoint the source of the noise, which grew louder and louder along with a whoosh of air that stirred the curtains behind them.

Trey yelled something and shoved her hard, sending her flying into the recesses of the stage. His body landed next to hers as a half dozen wood crates smashed to the floor around them, splinters of wood hurtling through the air. The flashlight sailed out of her hand and clattered to the floor, dousing the light.

Billows of dust whirled past her face, making her cough. She covered her mouth to keep out the filth as she sat up.

"What…what just happened?"

Trey was already on his feet, crouched low, peering into the darkness. "Boxes fell from the top of the pile. You hurt?"

"No." She clambered to her feet. "We were almost crushed."

"Yes, ma'am," he said.

She saw a dark trickle of blood on his arm. "You're bleeding."

He didn't even look at the wound, but continued to stare upward. "Scratched."

"Those boxes fell at just the right moment, didn't they?" she said.

"Or the wrong one."

Something in his voice alarmed her. "Do you think the earthquake destabilized them?"

"I think they had help." His gaze was still riveted to the catwalk above them.

"Trey," she said, her voice low. "Who would do that? Fred? Somebody else? What are you thinking?"

He shook his head and pulled her back into the covering folds of the curtain. "I'm thinking that we need to leave this theater right now."

"I'm not going without Antonia."

He straightened to his full height, a good head and a half taller. "She's probably gone already."

"I need to know for sure."

"No, you don't. You need to get out of here."

"Is that an order, Captain?"

"A strong suggestion," he muttered.

"And if I don't comply?"

"Then I will help you to do that." His eyes glittered in the darkness.

"You're not army anymore."

"No, ma'am. Just a carpenter, but I will see you to the exit, one way or another."

"If I don't cooperate, what do you intend to do about it?" She fired off the challenge, her gut tightening at the look that rose in his face.

He stood, feet slightly apart, hands loose at his sides. Though he kept his voice just above a whisper, every syllable was clear. "Sage, you need to leave this theater for your own safety. If I have to carry you out kicking and screaming, I am prepared for that contingency."

She heard the hardened resolution in his quiet voice. Dimples and charming drawl aside, she knew he would not hesitate, and she was no match for his size and strength. She would lose this battle.

But not the war.

"Fine. I guess I have no choice if you're going to be a bully."

He did not smile. "Great. Let's move."

Was he right that someone had helped those boxes to fall on them? The same person who'd found her trapped and left her? Swallowing a surge of fear, she crept behind him back the way they had come. Trey's body was wire-taut as he led them toward the stage door.

She peered past the proscenium arch into the rows of empty chairs. A flicker caught her eye.

"Trey," she whispered. "I just saw a light. Out there." She pointed.

"Might be Fred or maybe Derick has arrived," he whispered back.

"No, I'm sure it's Antonia." She called out. "Antonia? Is that you?" No answer. "Maybe she didn't hear me. I'm going to go check."

"No, Sage."

There was warning in his voice, but she didn't listen. Instead she darted ahead of him toward the stairs.

He was after her in a moment.

She pushed against the metal door as he put a hand on her from behind.

Her knees trembled, a shaking that spread throughout her body.

Confused, she pushed the door harder but the shuddering kept on, rippling through her body until she could hardly stand.

Fighting for footing, she looked at Trey, unable to see his face clearly.

Somewhere in the recesses of her mind, the realization hit.

Earthquake.

The floor bucked and rolled under her feet like a live thing.

Trey went down on his back as the wood gave way.

"Get out," he yelled. "Sage, get out now."

Suddenly he was snatched from her view.

She tried to reach out to him, but she was being tumbled about as the surface continued to undulate. The sound of distressed wood shrieked and groaned around her. That's when her mind put it together. This was the moment every Californian held in the back of their mind. The reality that was heightened by the 1989 Loma Prieta quake and captured in faded black-and-white photos from 1906.

This was the day scientists and doomsday broadcasters had predicted would come.

She heard the theater rattle around her, the beams coming loose from their supports, bits of plaster beginning to fracture and fall.

This was no ordinary earthquake.

This was the big one.

A sudden upheaval under her feet tossed her onto her back and she found herself staring at the ceiling, sections of which were breaking away, loosening huge chunks of plaster. She desperately tried to get her feet under her, to find some stability against the violent movement.

Somewhere she heard a scream. Antonia?

No time to process.

She wanted to call out for Trey, but the words froze in her throat as roar of sound enveloped her.

Like a scene from a bad movie, she watched uncomprehendingly as the floor of the stage ripped in half, sections parting wide like the jaws of a hungry beast.

A black chasm of splintered wood gaped in front of her and Sage rolled into the abyss, darkness swallowing her up.

FOUR

Trey tried to figure out which direction was up. His body filled with one desperate need. *Get to your feet, soldier.* Try as he might, he could not find a point of reference in the tumbling chaos. The thunderous shaking unleashed a tsunami of sound as wood and pieces of the old opera house ripped loose and smacked into him, bashing his shoulders and slicing into his neck. He threw up his hands to shield his head as his body finally made contact with what he assumed was the floor.

Another twenty seconds of tooth-rattling vibrations and the tumult was suddenly over. He sat up, loosening a pile of grit that showered off of him. He blinked hard. It was completely dark and for a moment he wondered if he had been knocked blind. Gradually, a weak filtering of light from somewhere up above made him realize that first off, he was not blind and second, wherever he'd fallen there would no longer be the easy comfort of a light switch.

"Sage?" he called. Trey had not felt fear since his return from the war zone, but he felt it now, thick and weighty, as he received no answer. He looked around, trying to get his bearings. He'd fallen through the stage, into this cavernous black space. Far above he could now make out the underside of the wood floor, ripped and jagged, showing through the clouds of dust that billowed everywhere. Perhaps she had not fallen with him. Maybe she was still up there. "Sage," he shouted again. The quiet was undisturbed.

He got to his feet, wobbling on the debris that slipped and slid beneath his feet. Every movement unleashed another tide of detritus and each sound made him stop, ears straining for some noise, any sign of life, from her. His heart hammered against his ribs as he floundered his way free, peering through the gloom to find her. *Where are you?* He prayed she was safe, that maybe she'd had time to run off the stage before it buckled. Yet another situation in which she would never have found herself if she'd listened to him in the first place. No time for quiet deliberation.

"Sage Harrington, answer me right now!" he bellowed in a volume so loud it echoed and bounced through the darkness.

It was not an answer, exactly, but a whoosh of debris stirred somewhere at his eleven o'clock. He scrambled over broken boards until he neared the spot, wishing he had not lost his grip on the flashlight earlier. He called again, treading gently on the rubble, turning over sheets of plaster until he saw a tiny pinprick of light. He got to his knees and pawed with his hands until he found the source, the luminous dial of Sage's watch. He grasped her slender wrist and pulled her arm free, shoving aside as much of the mess as he could until he unearthed her.

She was covered in dirt, eyes closed.

He pressed two shaking fingers to her throat.

At his touch she jerked awake and bolted backward, her feet scrambling for purchase, eyes wild and glittering in the gloom. "Don't touch me, don't touch me."

Trey held up his hands, palms forward. "It's me, Sage. Trey Black. I'm not going to hurt you."

The crazed sheen in her eyes did not abate. Panting, she scanned the ceiling as if expecting a weight to drop down from above at any moment. Her body began to tremble and a bead of sweat rolled down her forehead.

In the face of her reaction, his anger trickled away. He knew the look, he'd seen it before, long after the bombs had stopped and the bullets went quiet. He'd known good men to suffer from PTSD, even after they were safe at home, back with the people who had anguished over them their entire tour of duty. Maybe for some, there was no safety anymore after war imprinted that fear deep down inside. The realization added to the weight of grief he felt over what had happened to her, to them both, in Afghanistan. He tried again, softening his voice. "It's okay. There was an earthquake."

"An earthquake?" she parroted back in a whisper.

"Yes," he said. "We're in the Imperial Opera House. We were standing on the stage when it collapsed." She nodded and he took that as a good sign. "I wondered if you are hurt. Would it be okay if I came closer and checked you out?"

She might have nodded, he wasn't sure in the dark, but he approached slowly until he was near enough to get a better visual. She'd moved to a spot where the light from above was less obstructed and he could see enough to know she didn't have any open wounds that he could detect, except for a series of cuts on her face and hands. At his touch she flinched and tensed, so he stopped and smiled. "Just going to make sure there's nothing broken, okay?"

He tried again and this time she did not pull away so he moved his hands along her legs and arms, until he was satisfied that there were no bones massively out of place. It was impossible to discern if she'd sustained any internal injury or head trauma. He'd just have to pray she'd escaped those, too. By the time he was done with his makeshift medical exam, her breathing had normalized. She drew her knees up to her chest. His heart skipped a beat at how very young she looked, how very small and delicate against the yawning mass behind her.

"It was a big one."

"Yes. The Big One, I'd say." He could imagine the frenzy taking place on the city streets—fire crews, police and every available city employee working to salvage life and property. San Francisco was a modern city in every sense of the word, and it had the reinforced steel skyscrapers to show for it, but he'd seen enough of the old buildings during his morning runs to know that there would be plenty of destruction to deal with.

"We've got to get out," she said with only a slight tremble in her voice. "Will someone come to help us?"

"I think we'd be better off taking care of our own rescue," he said, seating himself on a chunk of broken bricks.

"Do you think Antonia fell, too? And Fred?"

"I haven't seen anyone but the two of us." No sign of whoever had pushed the boxes down on them. He looked up at the stage floor some twenty feet above them. What had probably been a set of two ladders leading up from under the stage area had been ripped away during the quake until only a few rungs were left clinging to the walls. All around them were piles of boxes, but most were smashed too badly to be of use helping them climb out.

Sage's breathing was steadier now. She patted her pockets and produced a cell phone, groaning as she peered at the cracked screen. "No signal here. It's completely useless. What about yours?"

"I don't carry a cell phone."

Her mouth fell open. "What kind of person doesn't carry a cell phone in this day and age?"

He shrugged. "The kind that doesn't want to be connected, I guess." He sighed. "In a war everyone has to be accounted for every moment, for their safety. I just…" He shook his head, wondering why in the world he was telling her this. "I wanted to disconnect, to sort of vanish for a while and remember who I used to be. Does that make sense?"

Her eyes shimmered and she gave a tiny nod. He wanted to cup her cheek just then, to make her understand that war had changed both of them, but the bite of anger stilled his hands. Her trauma had been totally avoidable. "Cell phone probably wouldn't help anyway, since we're basically underground, and even if we could call, the networks are probably jammed. Texting might be about the only option."

"I'll text Antonia now." She waited for a moment with no response.

"So this is going to be a do-it-yourself rescue," Trey said. "I'm going to poke around and see if there's an exit down here."

She got to her feet. "Me, too."

He was about to tell her she should remain seated, the memory of her earlier reaction haunting him, but something told him she did not want to be alone, even though it would kill her to say so. So be it. Her PTSD would be the unspoken elephant in the room. At least for now. He offered a hand and she took it, rising in a cloud of dust that made them both cough.

It was hard to access the perimeter of the room, blocked as it was by the ruins, but he found one section of brick that gave him a starting point. "We'll work our way around as best we can, and if there are no exits, we'll go to plan B." He began feeling his way along the rough brick.

"What's plan B?" Sage said, shuffling behind him.

"I don't know. I haven't come up with that yet."

She sighed and pressed closer to his back. He tried to ignore the way her presence made his breath tick up a notch as they climbed over boards and scraps of what looked like ancient theater backdrops.

"What's that?" Sage said, moving away from him. For a moment he lost track of her.

"Where are you?"

"Here," she said, flicking on a light that illuminated her smile. "I found the flashlight and it still works."

He couldn't help but return that smile. "That's one blessing working in our favor," he said.

Her smile dimmed. "No blessing. Just a happy coincidence."

He decided not to argue the point, but deep down he knew the truth. *Both of us just survived a massive earthquake and God tossed in a flashlight to boot.* Now it was up to Trey to get them both out of there.

"Let's move." He straightened his shoulders and pressed on.

Sage had to force her fingers to relax their death grip on the flashlight. Deep breaths. Anything to press away the fear she'd felt when she'd woken up buried, smothered and in darkness. She busied herself flicking the beam of light over the piles, assisting, being productive, not the helpless child she'd been a moment before. Not here. Not in front of him.

The thought shivered through her mind. They were both alive and intact, but Antonia might not have been so lucky. Sage had seen her enter the theater and head through the lobby, but where had she disappeared to? By the time Sage parked her car, Antonia was nowhere to be found and the woman had not responded to a single text or call. Maybe she'd departed again, decided against talking to Sage.

Sage was aggravated by the trembling in her knees. Part of her wished she was alone, without a witness to her struggles. The other part, a tiny part deep down in her soul, was grateful that Trey was with her to keep the darkness at bay. He did not deserve to be trapped in there with her, but she was glad not to be alone.

Lost in her thoughts, she did not notice that Trey had stopped until she plowed into him from behind, her cheekbone meeting his shoulder blade.

"What is it?" she asked, rubbing the feeling of him off her cheek.

"A door, I think, but it's covered by these broken beams. We're going to have to shift some things." He started to hurl some of the smaller pieces aside. She tried to help without losing her grip on the flashlight.

"Ouch," he said as she smacked him with the end of a beam.

"Sorry."

"Just hold the flashlight for a minute."

"And stay out of the way?" she snapped. "Don't order me around."

"I'm not ordering…" he began, an edge in his voice. "I'm asking you to please hold the flashlight while I work. If you want, we can take turns and you can haul wood and I'll hold the flashlight after a while."

She didn't answer, but she determined that no matter how messed up she was inside, she would not let Trey see her as weak. Holding the flashlight like a sword, she bit back the sassy remarks that circled in her brain.

Trey cleared enough that they could see the outline of the door fully now. It was wooden, partially decayed and splintering in some places. He grabbed the handle and yanked. It ripped away from the door, sending him stumbling back.

She kept her smile under wraps. "Here. Maybe we can pry it open with this." She passed him a thin metal rod, clammy with moisture.

He shoved it in the crack under the threshold and threw his weight against the iron bar. A section of wood crumbled. Tossing the bar aside, he grabbed the remaining door planks and exerted pressure. They pulled away easily.

Sage shone the flashlight into the corridor beyond.

"Where does this lead?" Trey said.

"I'm not sure. There are a series of tunnels that connect various storage rooms and such. Barbara said she'd send me the blueprint, but I never got anything."

He stepped into the dark interior, disturbing a fine layer of dust from the floor. It was quiet. Not the tiniest sound to indicate there was anyone else close by. He wondered if whoever had sent the boxes down on them hadn't survived the quake. Trey didn't allow himself further speculation. "Well lookee here," he called, disappearing into the tunnel and emerging a moment later carrying a ten-foot wooden ladder. "We may not have to chance the tunnel. This might be tall enough to reach up to the set of ladder rungs up there." He pointed to the slats that still clung, against all odds, to the side of the chamber where they had fallen.

She grabbed the rear end of the ladder and helped him carry it to a spot where he could unfold it properly. He gingerly climbed up a rung, testing the integrity of the wood.

"Will it hold?" she said.

"I guess we'll find out." He started up.

"What happens if you're ten feet up when it gives out?" she called to his back.

"Then you're going to want to make sure you're not standing underneath me," he called.

Sage rolled her eyes. Typical. If he fell down and smashed himself up, how would that change their situation for the better? And if someone bad was ready and waiting for Trey to emerge from the hole? Her breath grew short as she watched him climb higher, the wood slats creaking under his feet. Reaching the top, he stretched out his arms and grabbed hold of the other set of rungs. One snapped under his hand, sending a chunk of wood hurtling down.

"Look out," he shouted.

Sage dodged the falling piece. "It's rotten. Don't risk it."

"You're telling me not to take risks? That's a good one." He crept cautiously up the ladder.

Her stomach contracted. She was back in camp, an angry Trey Black arguing with his commanding officer's orders.

Too risky. No place for a civilian, a woman civilian. This is a war, not a photo op. Don't order me to do this.

But she'd used her connections and he'd been railroaded into taking her. Too risky? She'd fought hard to show him she was not afraid, and every bit as tough as he was.

What a joke.

And the cost of her bravado? Her foolish pride? Luis's life.

She swallowed a sudden lump in her throat, unaware that he was speaking again.

"What?" she called up.

"I said did you hear that?"

She refocused and listened hard. "No. Is it Antonia?" She wished she could risk climbing the ladder behind him, but their combined weight would collapse it for sure.

He was silent for a moment.

"What?" she yelled again. "What did you hear?"

"Quiet, I'm listening," he called down.

She would have socked him in the shoulder if he was closer. Instead she bit back her temper and remained silent, wondering if somewhere in the massive wreck he'd heard Antonia or Fred. If she was still the praying kind, she would ask God to make it so.

FIVE

The dust drifted past the gap in the ruined stage floor. He felt the urgent need to make a decision, but which one? Climb farther up, find the nearest exit and hope it was unblocked? Go back down, take the unknown tunnel and hope it led to an exit? Risk assessment didn't work too well when both options were equally bad. A faraway crack sounded somewhere. A gunshot? Or his ears fooling him? *Echoes from the past, Trey.*

"Did you hear Antonia?" Sage yelled. "You've got to get to her."

"I dunno what I heard," he said, his mind momentarily bringing up the toppled boxes that had nearly flattened them earlier. He could not escape the feeling that Antonia was not the only one hiding in the shadows, though he could not for the life of him imagine why. As the ruins shifted and packed down, there was a cacophony of tiny noises and it was impossible to tell if any were caused by human activity. No more time to chew on it. Up or down?

Neither option held enough certainty until he got more intel. He ascended one more rung on the aged ladder to better see into the gap. His foot broke through the wood. Grabbing at the rickety structure started a domino effect as the wood pieces snapped one by one, and he began to slide.

He heard Sage cry out from below, but he could not stop his downward momentum. He busted through several more slats before one held and he clung there, feet dangling into the black space below.

"Hold on," Sage yelled. "I'm moving the ladder."

Perspiration rolled down his temples as he hung there with clawed fingers, listening to the ominous crackle and groan of the wood as it took the punishment of his bulk. He felt a bump on his foot as Sage shoved the ladder as close as she could manage. A few wild swings of his feet nearly knocked it over.

"Stop thrashing," she commanded. "Straight down at your five o'clock. That's as close as I can get it with all this junk in the way down here."

He almost smiled at her commanding tone as he maneuvered into position and put both feet on the ladder. In a ridiculous, awkward fashion, he managed to transfer his weight and climb down as quickly as he could.

Wiping the sweat from his face with the back of his hand, he pulled a sliver of wood from his palm. "Thanks."

She stared up at the bits of tinder still clinging to the bricks. "Looks like we're not climbing out that way."

"Sorry," he said. "On to plan B, but there is some good news."

"I could use some right about now."

He walked around her and reached into a dusty alcove formed by a partially crushed piece of plaster. "I found my pack," he said, holding it up triumphantly. "I noticed it before the ladder let me down, so to speak."

She licked her dry lips and it made his heart hitch up a notch. Sighing, she looked up into the darkness. "I wonder what's going on up there, outside on the streets, I mean."

"It's not pretty, I'm sure." He thought about his brother, who was due to return to San Francisco that morning. Dallas was tough and resourceful, but he had some physical damage to work around. Trey pushed away that thought and the guilt that went along with it. He led the way back to the door they'd forced open. Cool air bathed his skin as he peered in.

"Let's go," Sage said, trying to edge around him.

"Hold up. I'm trying to think."

"What's to think about? It's our only way out, isn't it?"

"That's the problem. I'm not sure it is a way out. We could find ourselves at a dead end."

"Or we could find an exit, or Antonia. I say we get moving."

She had a point, though to his way of thinking, run in first and ask questions later was a great way to get killed. He endured a flare of anger at the realization that he found himself once again responsible for the safety and survival of Sage Harrington and her friend.

Not funny, God. I already failed that mission the first go-around. Isn't it somebody else's turn? Unfortunately, there didn't seem to be anyone else for him to hand over the task to.

"Take this," he said, opening a foil package from his pack and snapping a light stick to life. The green glow revealed her surprise.

"I thought you only carried around a hammer and screwdriver in there."

He took the flashlight from her and positioned himself in the front. "You'd be surprised what I squirrel away in this bag." He followed it up with a water bottle. "Drink sparingly, I've only got two."

Sage took the bottle and swigged some, her eyes closing in pleasure. He watched the fine muscles of her slender throat, pale and delicate, as she swallowed. "Thank you," she said, handing it back to him. He took a quick gulp and recapped it before they went inside.

The walls of the tunnel were brick, relatively intact except where the mortar had begun to crumble.

Here and there the floor was littered with chunks that had fallen away, and they had to move slower than he would have liked. He figured they were trekking south toward the rear of the theater, but as the tunnel turned and turned again, he could not keep his bearings.

Their combined light did not make substantial inroads into the darkness. He felt the familiar prickle, the tension about enemies lying in wait, and he was carried back to the day his team had done a routine sweep of a small village and walked right into a well-planned Taliban ambush. His memory reverberated with the rumble of tracer rounds, punishing machine-gun fire, the wail of a woman when she'd learned of her son's courageous death, their platoon medic who'd shown valor well beyond his years. So much death, so much fear. How unfair that it had followed him home. And her, too.

Sage must have been in the grip of her own anxiety because he noticed she pressed close to him, her hand brushing the small of his back at first, and then clutching a handful of his shirt. Trey stopped and beamed his light down at the floor. At the juncture where the floor met the wall was a small rectangular grate, no bigger than a shoebox, covered by an iron grille. A strange noise emanated from the spot, a thin whine. He dropped to his knees and peered in.

Sage knelt next to him. "What's in there?"

Trey flattened his body to the floor and pushed close until his face was practically touching the rusted metal. Now a mournful howl filled the tunnel and a tiny black nose pushed through the gap.

"It's Wally," Trey said. He curled his fingers around the grate and pulled.

Sage took the flashlight from Trey so he could use both hands. "How did he get there? I thought Fred was taking him."

"Don't think he got the chance. Wally's not too obedient. There must be a parallel tunnel or something," he grunted, yanking so hard on the metalwork that his teeth ground together. The bars did not give the tiniest bit. Wally continued to whine, louder. "I'll get you out, boy. I promise."

Trey returned to the outer room and retrieved the iron rod he'd used to pry his way through the tunnel doors. He sat down and began to heave at the bars.

Sage shook her head. "It won't work. We have to go on, Trey."

"I'm not leaving the dog," he said, gasping with the effort.

"He can find his way out."

He didn't answer. Instead he grabbed the hammer from his pack and a small chisel and tried to work at the corner hinges. When that proved unproductive he determined to use the last resort tool, brute force.

"Trey, this is ridiculous."

He ignored her and began to smash away at the edges of the grate with a hammer, sending bits of brick flying in all directions, hoping he didn't give the poor dog a heart attack.

"You need to stop." Sage gripped his shoulder midswing and he stood to face her.

"I'll be through in a few minutes if you'd quit interrupting."

Her mouth tightened. "We cannot waste time like this. Antonia is somewhere in there, and if there's someone after us, you're leading them right to our location."

He kept his voice level over his rising anger. "I told you, this will only take a minute. I'm not leaving this dog here."

"Trey," she snapped. "Big picture. We're trapped. Antonia may be hurt." She stabbed a finger at the grate. "That's a dog who can probably take better care of itself than we can."

The tide of anger burst through his reserve. "Listen up, Sage. I know it's a dog. And guess what? It's still a life and a precious one and I spent enough time with dogs in Afghanistan who risked their own safety to get us guys out of the pits we dug for ourselves."

"But…"

"And," he finished, his voice dangerously tense, "dogs are more loyal and selfless that some people I've met." He didn't wait to see her reaction but threw himself on the floor and took up the hammer again, drowning out any response she might have made with the ringing of steel on rock.

Sage leaned her back against the rough brick behind her, feeling like a child who has been taken to task. *More selfless than some people...* He would never understand that her mission in Afghanistan wasn't for her own personal comfort and enjoyment. And wasn't she paying the price for her time there? Emotionally crippled, caged by fear. He had no right to go ballistic on her for putting Antonia's life over the dog's.

She would go on without him, find her own way through the corridors. Six steps into the blackness and her skin began to prickle, her nerves jumping uncontrollably. *Come on, Sage. You're not afraid of the dark.* The truth rang mockingly in her head. She was, down to the depths of her soul, too scared to venture into the belly of the opera house on her own. Where was the intrepid woman she'd been? That woman had been slain right next to Luis in a split second of horror that now stretched out into a lifetime. She steeled herself against the tears that threatened.

Hating herself and the cowardice that shivered through her body, she returned just in time to see Trey slide the grate away from the wall and flatten himself in front of the hole.

"Wally," he called softly into the void. "Sorry about the noise, buddy. Come on out. It's okay now."

At first there was no sign of movement and Sage wondered if his efforts had been futile. It would serve him right and prove she was smarter than he gave her credit for. But something in his optimistic tone and the gentleness with which he shoved his big hands into the darkness made her hope that she was wrong.

Long minutes ticked by. Trey got to his feet and brushed off the knees of his jeans. "I think I scared him."

She wanted to put her arms around him, to forget the condemnation she'd heard in his tone a moment before and soothe the small grief that slumped his broad shoulders. "Dogs are clever," she said brightly. "Didn't you tell me that your brother wanted to be a kennel master in the marines?"

Trey nodded as he packed up his tools. "Yes, but that didn't pan out."

"Why?"

Trey's expression changed suddenly. He looked at the ceiling. "He got hurt." He cleared his throat. "Because of me. And that ended his chances to be a marine."

When he finally met her gaze she saw a world there in his eyes that she hadn't noticed before, maybe hadn't allowed herself to see. She reached a hand to him, to bridge the gap that seemed to have narrowed with his admission. "I…"

A scrabbling noise drew their attention. The rubble around the grate hole began to vibrate as if some determined gopher was tunneling in from the other side.

"Rats?" she said.

Trey grunted. "Oh, man, I hope not. I hate rats."

The rubble suddenly erupted in a shower of grit and Wally's tiny wedge of a head popped through the opening. He shook his head, ears flapping wildly as he looked around.

"Hey, Wal," Trey shouted, crouching to snag the little animal. The rest of Wally emerged, all long legs and whip of a tail, his sides heaving rapidly.

Trey tried to wipe the grime off the dog, but Wally would settle for nothing short of a complete tongue bath of Trey's cheeks. "All right, all right," he laughed, waving away the eager canine. "You can thank me later." He retrieved the water bottle and poured some into his cupped palm.

The dog lapped it up.

Sage knelt and peered into the hole while Trey examined the dog for wounds. "Wonder what's on the other side of this wall."

Trey didn't answer.

She turned to find him tense, face grave as he bent over Wally. "Can you get the towel out of my pack?" he asked.

Fueled by the gravity of his tone, she hurried to snatch it up and hand it to him. He pressed it carefully to the dog's side and then pulled it away.

"Is he hurt?" she whispered.

He held up the towel for her to examine with her glow stick. Her breath caught as she saw the dark stain. "Blood?"

He nodded and turned back to the dog, who kept wiggling out of his grasp. "Hang on." He fished in his pocket and pulled out a tiny cellophane package. "Can you hold one of these and see if he'll lick it while I try to stop the bleeding?"

She took the bag of saltwater taffy from him, unable to resist a grin. "You're still the candy man, aren't you?" She couldn't tell exactly, but she thought he might have blushed.

"Yeah, well I guess every man has his vice."

Even in a war zone, Trey was the one person who could be counted upon to have a stash of sweets collected from anywhere he could acquire it—packages from his mother, trades with the other soldiers and even some sugarcoated almonds he'd managed to score from a local villager. It amused her and Luis that the big, bold captain had the insatiable sweet tooth of a toddler. Her cheeks warmed when she remembered how he'd shared some partially melted toffees with her. Even in their mushy state, she'd never enjoyed a piece of candy as much as that mangled treat. Nothing had tasted as sweet since and she doubted anything ever would.

Shaking away the thought, she unwrapped a piece of yellow taffy and held it up for Wally, who held still long enough to sniff at it.

"Good stuff, Wally," she said. "Try a taste and see."

Wally shot out a slender pink tongue and gave a tentative lick. Then he set about sniffing the thing with his tiny jelly bean of a nose. One more half-hearted lick and then he lost interest, wiggling out of Trey's grasp and starting off to give the walls a thorough once-over.

"Sorry," she said, tossing the candy aside. "He doesn't have a sweet tooth." She'd gone for a teasing tone, a way to smooth things over between them, but he didn't answer her.

She came closer and saw he held the towel in his hands, staring at the stains. "Is he too hurt for you to help him?" She put a hand on his hard biceps, feeling the wash of shame at her earlier actions. "Maybe I can carry him while we look for a way out. If we wrap his wounds tight…"

"It's not that," Trey said. "Wally is perfectly fine, no wounds at all, anywhere."

"Fine? Then…"

He held up the blood-stained towel. "This isn't his blood."

SIX

Trey chewed a piece of orange taffy as they continued on, trying to keep his own worry in check. Sage's pace was brisk behind him; he'd seen in her face the tide of fear rising higher and higher as her mind put the facts together. The proof was there in ugly dark swirls on the towel. Someone most definitely was trapped in the Imperial, and whoever it was needed help. Fast.

Trey found he was moving so quickly Sage was now panting to keep up. He slowed and they continued through the brick corridor, Wally scampering along next to them. Another five meters and the tunnel pinched off into two. They stood at the juncture, lights shining down both passages, once again faced with a decision.

Sage held up her hands. "The air feels a little cooler on this side," she said, pointing to one of the openings. "Or maybe I'm just imagining it."

He tried to check with his own hands but could

detect no difference. "Cooler could mean there's an exit, or that it leads farther underground."

She hugged herself. "I don't know."

He noticed she was shivering and he wondered if she was succumbing to PTSD. He wrapped an arm around her shoulders and squeezed gently. "We'll get help soon."

Her head dropped onto his shoulder and then, suddenly, she turned to bury her face in his chest. He laid his cheek on the top of her hair, marveling at the electric shocks that prickled his whole body.

"Antonia could be dying," Sage whispered, her voice thick. "Dying alone and frightened."

He rubbed his hands over her back in slow circles, like his mother used to do when he was a small boy. "We'll find her."

Sage pulled away suddenly, glittering tears marking trails down her face. "But you can't promise that. She could be dead." She snapped her fingers. "Dead just like that and there's nothing you could do about it."

He knew Sage was no longer talking just about Antonia. "Like Luis?"

Her lip quivered. "All the weapons and planning and top-trained U.S. Army soldiers, and he is still dead."

Yes, Luis had died, just like that, and Trey hadn't been able to lift a finger to change that fact. He let her go and stood to face her, ready to take the full weight of her fear and outrage while keeping his own anger in check.

"You're right. We had weapons, planning, training and yet, we were still just a group of guys, led by another guy who did the best he could. Maybe there was something else I could have done to save Luis, but I did not have the skills, or the intuition or the savvy to sense what was going to happen. He died and I will never forget that I could have, should have, done more. I've felt the same for every wounded man, every casualty that happened under my watch, especially a civilian. Does it make you feel better to hear that?"

She stared at him. "You believe Luis never should have died. It's my fault that he was there in the first place."

Trey started to speak and the words trailed away.

"Say it," she said, her voice vibrating with emotion. "Say it out loud."

"You didn't fire the bullet that killed him, Sage."

"That's a cop-out. Come on, Captain Black." Her fingers balled into fists. "Say what you've been dying to say. Tell me straight."

He picked up his pack. "No time for this now. We'll try one tunnel for a while and turn back if necessary."

She pulled at his shoulder, fingers clawed. "You think it's my fault."

He shook her off, angry at being cornered. So

like her to demand an answer, even one she didn't want to hear. "Let it go."

She stepped in front of him. "I won't. I can't."

"Yes, you can," he hissed through gritted teeth. "This is pointless. Stop it."

She pressed her hands against his chest, forcing him to stop or plow right over her. His veins throbbed. "Sage, this conversation is over."

"Tell me, unless you're too much of a coward." Her eyes glittered, mouth hard. "I'm man enough to take it."

His self-control snapped. "Yeah, you are. You were always tougher than anyone, you knew better than the soldiers who lived and died in that camp and you definitely thought you knew more than me, didn't you? You forced yourself into an unsafe situation and Luis died. That's it."

She kept her palms there, but now the fingers curled themselves into the fabric of his T-shirt. Her face was dead pale in the gloom. "I...I killed him."

He grabbed her fists, wishing he could take back the words. "No. The enemy killed him. Luis was a grown man and he made his own choice to be there and he died because that's what happens in a war."

"He didn't want me to go alone." Her voice trembled. "He went because I wanted it."

"Listen to me," he said, pulling her to him as his own anger slipped away. "There's no blame. It's one of those things that happens because the world is troubled and broken."

"No blame?" A single tear slid down, shimmering on her cheek before it fell away into darkness. "Yes, there is, Trey. I can see it in your eyes." She pulled loose and turned her back on him, wiping her sleeve across her face as she hurried away.

Feelings pinwheeled through him—regret, sorrow, guilt. "Sage…things happen, terrible things, and war is the worst of all of it," he found himself saying.

She continued on, shutting out any comfort he offered. The phrases tumbled suddenly out of his mouth before he realized. *"In this world you will have trouble,"* he shouted after her. *Trouble* was an understatement. The memory came faster than he could shut it out. Trey behind the wheel of a getaway car while his gang brothers busted up a storefront and left their burning bandanna in front of the ruins. They hadn't seen what Trey saw, the store owner hiding in the shadows across the street, head bowed and a little boy tucked behind him. The boy looked at Trey, large eyes filled with a question.

Why?

Trey discovered in that moment, he had no answer. He did not know his own face in the rearview mirror, nor his hands on the steering wheel. The world had sucked him in and morphed his soul into something unrecognizable even to himself.

The words of John 16:33 echoed wildly, the words he'd clung to since the day he'd discovered that the world had beaten him, the week he'd snuck back to the shopkeeper's store and helped sweep up the glass and board up the windows before he'd headed to the recruiter's office. It was a verse he still pored over when he felt as if his heart would break, lost in the darkness like he was at that very moment. *"But take heart, I have overcome the world,"* he finished softly.

Though he thought she hadn't heard, she stopped and turned. "This girl lost," she whispered. "And the world won."

He had to look away from the defeat on her face. "I've been where you are. Please, Sage. Listen to me," he whispered.

But she was already gone.

Sage could not stop her self-recrimination.
You were always tougher...
You knew better...
You forced yourself into an unsafe situation...
And Luis died, her mind supplied. She was not surprised at Trey's condemnation because she'd thought it herself in the terrible moments when her thoughts returned to the past. Somehow, hearing him say it aloud drilled it deep into her soul, past the numb void and into the tender part that was still capable of feeling. Luis had gone to Afghanistan

because of her. In his late fifties, he was no longer interested in capturing that sizzling headline that would make his career. His thoughts revolved around sweeter things; his grandchildren, church picnics and traveling the world after his retirement. One more job he'd do, for her. Because he knew how badly she wanted it. Because he was a friend of her father's from back in the Vietnam days.

Because he was a good man.

She reached up to wipe her face and found there were no more tears there. She was once again sinking into that numb void where the feelings couldn't reach her. Cold seeped through her bones.

Wally sniffed hard at a section of the tunnel a few feet in front of them. His tiny paws worked at the crumbling brick and he barked once, a high-pitched burst of noise that yanked her from her reverie.

She shone her light for a better look and Trey caught up and added his light.

"Sage…"

She could not stand the softness in his tone, the note of pity held there. It was better that they were antagonists, or two strangers working to find an escape. "Wally's found something," she said sharply. She heard him sigh and then he ran his hands along the brickwork.

"Used to be a door, I think, but it's been sealed

over." He scratched the dog behind the ears. "Sorry, Wally. No way through there."

Wally continued to whine and scrape at the spot, and Sage put her hand to the surface. She gasped. "Feel this," she said, grabbing his hand and guiding it next to hers.

After another few seconds they both felt it, a vibration as something struck the wall from the other side. One tremor, another.

"Someone is banging on the wall," Sage said. She immediately slapped her own hands against the brick until Trey handed her the flashlight.

"Try this."

She struck at the brick with the metal handle and pressed her palm there to feel for a response. Seconds ticked into minutes and there was no answering clang.

"What happened?"

Trey shook his head. "Maybe they had to move, things became unstable."

She stood back and examined the wall, which looked exasperatingly solid. "How can we break through it?"

Trey looked off down the tunnel. "We can't."

"We have to, there's someone alive on the other side, Antonia or Fred." She whacked on the wall again, hard enough to send a tiny chip of brick zinging through the air. A few moments later she was panting with nothing to show for it. She looked for Trey, annoyed that he hadn't added his strength to her efforts.

"You went nuts on the bricks before to get Wally out," she snapped. "You can't help me get to Antonia?"

He gave her a scathing look. "It's solid and you know it. We need another plan."

She rolled her eyes. "We've already tried plan B."

"Would you hush up a minute and look." He pointed to the top of the wall where a missing brick had left a neat rectangular impression.

"I don't see anything."

He guided her to his side and wrapped an arm around her shoulders. Though she didn't want to be anywhere close to him, her senses responded to his warmth, her own body molding to his. "There," he said, wiggling the flashlight beam at the space which she now saw was stuffed with twigs.

"It's a bird nest," he said. "Recently used. This area must get some sun during daylight hours."

"So this tunnel leads out?"

He released her and grabbed his pack. "There's only one way to find out."

Sage made a move to follow, but she felt the desire to return to the bricks. Even though she knew the person on the other end could not hear her, she put her fingers there and called out, "We'll be back to get you. I promise."

She found Trey looking at her and she felt her face flush. "I know they can't hear, I was just…"

He smiled. "No need to explain to me. I've run up against plenty of brick walls in my day."

She fell into step next to him and found herself asking the question. "How did you get through them?"

"Some I didn't because I wasn't meant to, but God helped me knock the others down. I've got plenty I'm still working on, believe me."

She felt a swirl of discomfort. She'd decided in the months following Luis's death that she did not want anything further to do with God. Before the incident, she'd been what she liked to term a "casual believer." He was in charge of the universe, but not in charge of her life. Now, there was no way she would invite God in. Period.

Looking to avoid any further conversation, she sped up the pace, noting that the tunnel seemed to slope upward. Perhaps it was her imagination, but she thought the blackness was lightening to gray.

Trey hastened faster, calling to Wally who lingered behind. They made another sharp turn. High up near the ceiling was a half-moon through which shone a slice of dusky light. Sage ran forward and looked into the space. "It's a storm drain or something. I can see up to the street."

"Here," he said, cupping his hands to give her a boost.

She stepped into his palms and he lifted her up until her chin was level with the stone edge. The alley was washed in long shadows from the setting sun. "It's the side street to the Imperial. I think I can see part of the deli." Her heart sank. "The road is covered with debris and there's glass everywhere."

"Do you see anyone?"

"No." She pushed herself higher and shouted into the gap. "Hey, we're trapped down here! Can somebody help?"

He continued to hoist her until she was able to put her feet on his shoulders. More of the ruins came into view and she heard the far-off wail of sirens. A set of trousered legs appeared and Sage shouted again.

The legs bent and Derick Long's face peered into the space. "Sage?"

"Yes, it's me and Trey Black."

Derick's eyes widened. "What a relief. I thought you'd been killed." He called to someone else and suddenly there were two sets of hands pulling at the drain cover until it gave way along with a row of bricks. Arms reached in to haul Sage out.

"Take Wally," Trey called.

Derick grunted in surprise as Trey lifted the little dog into Sage's hands before he himself was helped out of the tunnel. Derick clasped her in a hug. "I've been going bananas up here."

Sage blinked to adjust to the sensation of cool, misty air against her face. With Wally still cradled in her arms she did a slow scan of the surroundings. A chasm two feet across had opened up in the middle of the road, sucking down a portion of the sidewalk and several cars. The little salon across the street which was of newer construction stood seemingly undamaged, but the smaller brick buildings on either side were knocked cockeyed, their side walls separated from the main structure. Broken glass spangled the streets like fallen stars, glittering in the failing light. Two blocks farther up a police car and a fire truck were attempting to deal with the downed electrical wires that powered the trolley buses. She could hear the shouts of the emergency workers. It looked as though she had emerged into a war zone. Her head spun.

Derick led her to a section of undamaged sidewalk and forced her to sit, handing her a water bottle from which she drank before cupping her palm and letting Wally drink his fill. She caught Trey watching her and felt her cheeks pinking.

Trey briefed Derick and the other man who assisted in pulling them free, the owner of the deli across the street. They shouted to the officer working on the electric wires and he waved, face sweaty and expression grim, shouting back that he would be there as soon as he could. She stared out over the ruins and found her eyes damp. "It looks like a battleground," she whispered.

Derick nodded. "Radio said most of the phone lines are jammed. Masonry started raining down so we took cover, but the front doors are blocked. We were trying to find another way in."

Sage was about to ask Derick to explain the "we" when Rosalind hurried up along with the cop. Her blond bob was coated with the dirt that thickened the air and Sage was surprised to find that the woman was actually a few inches shorter than she remembered. That is until she realized Rosalind was wearing leather boots instead of the heels she'd had on the first time they'd met. She blew out a breath.

"The officer didn't want to come," she said with an annoyed glance at the cop. "But I told him you two needed medical attention."

"I'm Sergeant Rubio." He eyed Trey and Sage with a raised eyebrow. "Are you injured?"

"No, sir," Trey said. "But there is a chance of one victim, possibly two, trapped inside."

Rosalind started. "Who?"

"Fred Tipley was in there."

Rosalind blew out a breath. "No, he left just after I arrived. I got here just before the big quake. Fred called and demanded that I come." She raised an eyebrow at them. "He was pretty annoyed that you two insisted on staying inside to find Antonia, but he said he wasn't about to risk his neck trying to save you. He was more interested in what happened to Wally, so I told him I'd keep an eye out for him and stay here until we made sure you were all okay, and he left."

"Sage believes Antonia Verde was inside as well," Trey finished.

"Antonia," Derick cried. "What was she doing in there?" His eyes narrowed. "I thought you hadn't seen her."

Sage kept her voice light. "I wasn't sure. I saw her go in, but she may have left, too, as soon as the first shock hit. Trey and I looked, but we couldn't find her."

Rosalind looked closely at Trey. "Fred was right. The place was extremely busy for an abandoned opera house. Why were you in there after hours, Mr. Black?"

"Call me Trey, ma'am." He explained about Wally.

Rubio listened to a crackling message on his radio. "I can't take any more time for this. You're all safe and uninjured, so you've got to stay out of this area and let me do my job. I'll get a search team in there as soon as there's one free."

Derick stiffened. "I'm not leaving here with my employee possibly trapped in there."

"I'm sorry, but we're doing the best we can for

everyone right now. This Ms. Verde may or may not still be inside."

"Someone is," Trey countered. "We found blood. And…" he looked at Sage. "We thought there was someone else in there, someone who wanted us out."

He shook his head. "Out is a good idea. We'll send people in when we can. For now, you need to leave."

His tone brooked no argument. He watched as they walked around the massive crack in the road to the other side of the street where the deli owner, a mustached man named Jerry, ushered them to a bench outside his shop.

"Not much damage to my store except the windows," he said. "You can stay here. You're hungry."

He did not phrase it as a question before he disappeared inside to find them something to eat.

Rosalind crouched down and stroked Wally's dusty fur. "Poor little guy," she said, a catch in her voice.

Sage thought Wally looked much smaller out here, dwarfed by piles of rubble. "I'm surprised Fred would leave without him."

"Me, too," Rosalind said, "but I've never been able to figure Fred out. I'm a cat person, but maybe I'll have to make an exception for you until we can get you back to your owner." She pulled him into her lap where he lay for a few moments, enduring the petting before he hopped back down to the sidewalk, nose twitching at the smell of food.

Jerry returned with bowls of pierogi, little dumplings filled with cheese. Sage did not think she could eat anything, but the aroma carried along by the steaming delicacies made her mouth water. Trey, Sage, Derick and Rosalind devoured the food eagerly as Jerry looked on. Even Wally enjoyed lapping up several of the succulent treats. Jerry spooned up a bowl for two other shop owners who brought their own contributions—grape juice, sliced bread and a bag of tortilla chips. It was a strange combination, but no one complained.

Sage smiled at Jerry when he brought blankets and coffee. "How can we ever thank you enough?"

He waved her discomfort away. "I was here for the Loma Prieta Quake in '89. When my store flooded, people helped me, took care of me until I could open up the deli again. Now it's my turn to do the same for you."

She was overwhelmed at the kindness of this man who had been a total stranger not long before.

Evening shadows crept along the street and the small group sat talking in the eerie pool of lantern light. Shirlene, a heavyset lady from the hair salon, sat patiently while another woman applied a new bandage to the wound on her head.

Rosalind held the sterile wrap while the lady cut the first aid tape to fasten it into place. "Are you going to evacuate? I heard the police saying they wanted everyone to go."

Shirlene shook her head, making her double chins wobble. "It's all I have. There's no way I'm leaving my shop unattended."

She repeated the same thing to the cop when he returned just before midnight.

He looked too tired to argue, shifting his gaze to Sage and Trey. "We've got a partial building collapse, the old folks' home six blocks from here. Every available body is working that right now."

Sage felt her heart squeeze. Alone and trapped. She knew the feeling. She wondered in that moment if every person fights on their own personal battlefield. Brick walls, as Trey would say. She envied him the comfort God provided. She felt a flicker of desire to experience that sweetness for herself, but she shrugged away the thought and pulled the blanket Jerry had loaned her tighter around herself.

Rubio wiped his forehead and resettled the cap over his sweaty hair. "I'm going to level with you. It will be dawn by the time I can get people here, if then."

"That might be too late," Sage said.

"I'm sorry. Right now we can't risk the lives of rescuers going in there after a possible victim when we have plenty of confirmed injured to deal with."

"So you're going to turn your back on them," she said bitterly.

Trey took her arm to calm her which only made her more upset. She jerked away from him. "I'll go in myself, then."

The cop stood, feet planted. "No, you won't," he said. "We've taped it off and no one is going in there."

"You don't care," she said, choking on the words.

"Listen," he snapped. "I've got a dozen elderly people who can't even stand, let alone get themselves out. I just came from a dance studio where six kids were learning how to tap dance when their roof caved in." He paused and cleared his throat. "One of those kids didn't make it. Did you ever have to tell a parent that kind of news?" He stared at her, eyes dull with grief. "Don't tell me I don't care."

Sage's anger died away and shame took its place. This man was not her enemy. "I'm sorry."

He nodded wearily. "I'll be back tomorrow as soon as I can spare a team. Keep out of that opera house. As a matter of fact, it would have been smarter to evacuate, but that's going to be dangerous in the dark so you'd better stay here."

Derick looked up and down the ruined street. "Going to be a long, cold night."

Shirlene chimed in, "I've got a room behind the salon. There's a cot and a sofa for the ladies if you want to sleep there."

"We couldn't displace you," Rosalind said.

Shirlene laughed. "You're not displacing me. I've got a recliner in the front so I can keep a sharp eye out. My little shop is safe, but if there's another quake we'll be outside in a jiffy."

"I don't have such a good setup," Jerry said, chewing on an enormous dill pickle. "But you men can sleep in my delivery truck. Smells like pastrami, but there are worse things."

Trey smiled. "True story. That would be great. Thank you."

Derick did not look overly cheerful about the prospect, but he nodded.

Jerry went into the store with Derick to fetch blankets while Shirlene directed Rosalind inside the salon. Sage watched the ruined street sink into darkness. Looking up, she could not even see the stars through the thick veil of fog that rolled across the sky. She started to shiver, overwhelmed by frustration and the fear that the ground under her feet would fail her. At any moment the balance of her life could shift again without so much as a warning. She hated the uncertainty.

She felt a strong set of arms encircling her as Trey brought her close. "Cold?"

How had he known she longed for a tender touch to remind her that she was still alive? She did not think about it or consider the reasons she did not want Trey Black in her life. Instead, she gathered comfort from his embrace and leaned into the muscled strength of his chest. "A little."

"It was a really tough day today," he murmured into her hair. "Tomorrow will be better."

"But what if Antonia is trapped in there?" she whispered. "There could be more quakes."

"We'll have to take it one day at a time."

Jerry exited the store and settled into a patio chair, carrying a large ball of nubby yellow yarn and a half-knitted scarf. A shotgun sat across his lap.

"In case there's looting," Trey said in her ear.

She closed her eyes. What had happened to San Francisco? It was as if the destruction and desperation of her time in Afghanistan had somehow followed her here to America. She felt sick.

"Trey…" She turned to find that the perfect contours of his face disarmed her and she looked away for a moment. She lowered her voice to a whisper. "I still think Antonia is the only one who will tell me the truth about my cousin."

He squeezed her hand and leaned close, his warmth caressing her cheek. His chin was shadowed now, and the beginnings of a dark beard whisked against her skin. "If she's in there, we'll find her."

Her voice caught. "She could be dead already."

He stroked her back. "We'll get her out tomorrow. That's all we can do for now. Besides," he said, speaking low into her ear. "Maybe I can get some information out of Derick about your missing cousin since we're bunking in the same truck tonight."

There was a slight tone of derision in Trey's voice and she wondered what he thought about the handsome actor. She tried to search his face in the darkness. "You'd do that for me? Why?"

He hesitated, his eyes searching hers. "I'm not totally sure, but I feel like it's the right thing to do."

The right thing. She marveled at the thought of knowing what the right choice might be at any given time. He was so certain of himself, like she used to be.

Abruptly, she pulled away, the cold air rushing to remind her of the loss of his warm touch.

"Good night, Sage," he said, and she felt him watching her as she made her way into the salon.

SEVEN

Trey carried a musty blanket that smelled of cured meats and an exhausted-looking Wally, whose small body could not jump into the vehicle unassisted. The truck floor was cold, the space lit only by a small flashlight Derick held to light Trey's way as he climbed in and deposited Wally and the blanket.

"Mind if I keep this open a little?" Trey said, wedging a board under the roll-up door. Tunnels were one thing, but he couldn't see shutting himself into a windowless metal container if he could help it. There was a reason he'd never gone for tank duty. Little metal box, one way out.

"Absolutely. Honored to be sharing a truck with you this evening, Captain Black." Derick grinned. "You can regale me with stories from the war."

"Don't think so." Those stories were kept close to the vest, shared only with people who could understand, military brothers, not trotted out for cocktail-party talk.

"It would be better than my endless stories about show business, believe me."

Derick helped him spread out the blanket, which annoyed him further. He handed Wally to Derick to give him something to keep him busy and the actor accepted the wriggling bundle as if it was a live grenade.

"These are odd circumstances," Derick said.

"Affirmative. Was there much damage to your place?"

"No. We did a massive retrofitting of the estate after Loma Prieta. Not so much as a crack in the plaster. I beelined down here as soon as the shaking stopped, but I had to leave the Bentley and walk most of the way because the streets are impassible toward the center of town."

Cool air filtered in through the gap, but Trey did not mind. He'd vowed in Afghanistan that he would never again take America's gentler climate for granted. He retrieved Wally and put the dog on the blanket before he lay down himself and Derick settled in on his own pile of bedding. "Were you able to get any calls out?"

"No. Just a text to my wife, Barbara."

Trey stiffened, keeping his tone casual. "Did she respond?"

He sighed. "Not yet." Derick let the light play upward to the metal beams. "She's…not communicative at times."

"Surely she'd answer back knowing you'd just been through a massive earthquake."

"She'll probably check in as soon as she hears the news, but she can get lost in her own world."

Trey looked for a way to keep the conversation going. "She'll be happy the Imperial is still standing."

"Barely. It was hardly standing before."

"Going to be expensive to repair."

Derick shifted. "Let's be honest, Captain. That wreck is never going to be repaired. I could hand over every penny from every movie I've ever made into that sinkhole and it wouldn't make a dent. This earthquake was the nail in the coffin." His words were dark but the tone was almost cheerful. "Too bad we don't have earthquake insurance. Just fire."

"So why lead her on? Why let her hire people to fix it up?"

He considered the question for a moment. "Because it makes her happy."

"Until your money runs out?"

"I was hoping something would happen before then."

"What exactly?"

"I don't know," he said, his voice easy and charming, as if he was reciting lines for a show. "Things usually break my way. I've never been the long-range planner. I see something and I take it. Rosalind will tell you I have no mind for business." He laughed. "You know, I'm going to talk about this idea with my agent. Young hero trapped in the wake of a massive earthquake. Must struggle to save his small band of travelers including a lovely woman photographer."

Trey wasn't thrilled that Derick thought of Sage as lovely. For some reason, it galled him. The flashlight caught the lines on Derick's face, the shadows that aged his eyes and stripped away the sheen of youth. *You're too old to be the young hero.* Trey was ashamed of himself for enjoying the notion.

Derick seemed lost in thought. "I used to imagine that I'd been on the plane that crashed and killed my parents. I would smash my way into the cockpit and bring that plane safely to the ground with accompanying swashbuckling music and flattering camera angles, of course."

Trey was unsure how to respond. "How old were you?"

"Eighteen, just starting out in the modeling biz, thanks to my mother, working at a pizza shop at night. Probably best that my father didn't live to see my acting career take off. He was a senator, you know, and didn't believe in sharing his wealth with a son who hadn't earned it. Despised show business and would have had a coronary at my first role, which was on a soap opera. He wanted me to be an engineer." Derick laughed again. "Can you picture me as an engineer?"

Trey couldn't. "Maybe when you retire."

"Nah. When I retire, I'm going to restore boats. I'm working on a wooden beauty from the 1920s right now. Combination of oak and mahogany that would make you weep."

"Sounds expensive."

Derick looked at him sharply and then smiled. "I can afford it. Looking at a couple of movie deals right now. What about you? Carpentry pay well?"

Trey recognized the gibe. "Nope, but that's okay. I just want to build a cabin in the mountains. I don't need a boat." *Or a mansion, or a Bentley.*

Derick looked honestly interested and Trey had no idea if the guy was a better actor than he'd imagined or he really was the easygoing pal he portrayed. "Sounds perfect. A quiet life in the mountains. I'd probably go nuts without people around, but it sure has its appeal." He jerked and pulled his phone from his pocket. "Text."

"From Barbara?"

Derick peered at the tiny screen. "No. Nothing important. Not from Barbara." He bid Trey a goodnight and turned his back toward the opposite wall of the truck.

Trey could see the flicker of light as Derick texted. Nothing important? He didn't buy that for a moment.

With his head propped on a stack of flattened cardboard boxes, Trey listened to the sound of sirens and wondered how many people lay trapped, praying for rescue. He remembered with a surge of sadness how slowly the minutes had ticked away when he and Sage had waited for a medic to treat Luis. Rescue hadn't come then in spite of heroic efforts by the medic and Trey's own anguished prayers.

He hoped that if Antonia really was trapped in the opera house, she would have the strength to make it until morning.

Sage must have drifted off into sleep somewhere in the hours before dawn as exhaustion won out over the fear of another quake. It was still dark when she sat up, eyes bleary and mouth dry, heart beating hard as the disorientation ebbed away. *There was a massive earthquake, and I'm in a hair salon.* Her mind added one more bit of absurd information.

Trey Black is sleeping in a delivery truck just outside my door.

It must all be some sort of bizarre dream. The fact that Trey was back in her life was enough to throw her off balance without a catastrophic earthquake tossed in. For a moment, she wanted to bury her head under the blanket and wish it all away, but the anxious stirring in her gut would not allow it.

Rosalind's bed was empty and she found her talking to Shirlene in the front room that looked out onto the ruined street, quiet and empty in the cold morning. Rosalind was examining the little bottles of nail polish in the store window, righting the fallen ones and sliding them into precise rows like colorful soldiers.

"My mother used to do nails, but I don't remember her having nearly this many colors to choose from." Looking at Sage, Rosalind said, "Did we wake you?"

"No. I'm surprised I slept at all."

Rosalind herself looked rumpled, her black jacket streaked with dirt. "Didn't sleep much either. Kept dreaming the floor was shaking. I don't know if those were real aftershocks or my imagination. Hungry?"

Sage shook her head. "No, just thirsty."

Shirlene handed her a cup of water. "The pipes aren't working, but this is from a bottle in the fridge. It's not too cold anymore 'cause there's no electricity."

Sage gulped the water while Rosalind paced in front of the window. "I wish I had my bike. I could see if Antonia headed back to the guest house."

"The police should be here soon," Sage said, eyeing the gray streaks in the sky that meant dawn must be approaching. She hoped it was true, that they had people to dedicate to a wrecked opera house in the face of such enormous need.

Shirlene fiddled with a battery-powered radio

until she zeroed in on a tinny voice. "Initial estimates of the earthquake calculate the magnitude as a 7.9 on the Richter scale. Reports are coming in now of a partial collapse at the Bay City Mall where rescuers are working around the clock to free some of the estimated two dozen people trapped in the wreckage. Bystanders are assisting in the frantic efforts. Traffic movement around the city is at a standstill due to road failures, disabled stoplights, the collapse of the Geneva Avenue overpass and the damage to the Central Viaduct of Highway 101."

Here the reporter paused. When she continued on, she sounded tired, as if she too had spent the night waiting for the next catastrophic shaker to occur. "Receiving word now of extensive damage in the Marina District. More in a moment."

Shirlene sighed. "Our poor San Francisco."

Rosalind continued to pace. "Not surprised about the Marina District. It's all built on landfill. I tried to tell Derick and so did Barbara when he bought a waterfront condo there. He's going to be crushed if anything happened to that silly boat of his."

Sage tried to push away the tragic news and focus on Rosalind. "Derick didn't listen to Barbara?"

Rosalind waved a hand. "Derick doesn't listen to anyone, really." She laughed grimly. "His head is in the clouds and it's nearly impossible to bring him back to earth sometimes."

Sage stepped closer, interrupting the path of Rosalind's pacing. "When was the last time you talked to Barbara?"

Rosalind stopped, blinking. "Can't quite remember."

Odd, for a woman who Sage knew kept every detail of Derick's business life in order. "You can't remember?"

Rosalind's eyes met hers. "I tried to stay out of Barbara's and Derick's personal lives. I'm their business manager and I like to keep it that way."

"Were they having problems?"

She shook her head. "Their marriage is their business, and I'm no therapist." Her eyes narrowed in accusation. "I'm not a gossip columnist, either."

The criticism was a fair one. "I'm not interested in gossip. I need to know where Barbara is, to speak with her."

Rosalind's tone softened. "Sorry. I know your motives are good, but you're a photographer and they can be real lowlifes when they're trying to get the dirt on a star. I forgot for a moment that you're one of the good guys." Rosalind blinked. "Aren't you?"

Sage knew from Barbara that their personal lives were fair game for paparazzi so she let it go and posed the question flat-out. "Do you know where Barbara is?"

"Ask Derick."

Sage stood as tall as she could, but she was still a few inches shorter than Rosalind. "You can't tell me?"

"I already did, but you don't seem to accept my answer. She's in New Mexico, as far as I know. I can see that you think I'm lying but really, what would be the reason? I just manage the books and that's a lot easier when Barbara is around, frankly. She's a stabilizing influence. She's got a good head for business. Derick is no help with it."

"I should have heard from her by now. It's not like her to disappear."

"Maybe you don't know her like you think you do."

"What's that supposed to mean?"

Rosalind sighed, wiping at a smudge on her cuff. "Nothing. Sage, there's no dirty plot afoot here, at least not on our end. Barbara made plans to go to Santa Fe and I have no reason to believe she's doing anything but enjoying her vacation, probably the last time she'll have much of a vacation with twins on the way."

"It's a weird time for her to travel."

Rosalind shuddered. "I know. If it were me, I wouldn't show my face in public. Her belly is enormous." She looked sheepish. "Sorry. That was mean. No filter." Rosalind paused for a moment. "Did Barbara tell you anything? I mean, about how things were going with Derick? Is that why you're worried?"

"No. Why?"

She shrugged. "Just curious. I don't understand those two at all."

They faced off for a moment, each woman measuring the other. Sage respected Rosalind for not wanting to talk about her boss's personal life. Unless it was not respect at all, but her way of covering up for the fact that someone had made Barbara disappear. A nerve flared deep inside, telling her that Rosalind was not revealing all she knew.

The reporter on the radio started up again, listing the catalogue of fatalities. Rosalind waved a hand and opened the door. "I can't stand to hear any more. This is too depressing. I'm going outside for some air."

After sending another half dozen texts to Antonia and trying her cell phone again with no answer, Sage checked the time; nearly five o'clock. She shivered against the cold whispering in through the open door. She wondered how comfortable it had been for Trey and Derick. The walls seemed to move closer, pressing the tiny space around her. One more tremor and maybe the salon would come tumbling down around them, too. She was making for the door when Shirlene handed her an oversize San Francisco Giants sweatshirt. "Black isn't your color, I'm sorry to say, but it's warm."

"Thank you," Sage said, wondering again at the kindness of this stranger. Would she herself have been so willing to share with someone she didn't know? Shame weighed heavy in her stomach. No, because she did not trust people anymore, did not see the good in anyone through the heavy cloak of depression. She wanted to say something else that would communicate the depth of her gratitude, but Shirlene was sweeping her little shop, picking up the bottles of hair color and foils that had scattered after the quake. Sage let herself out and gently closed the door behind her, pulling on the comforting heft of the sweatshirt.

The street was still dark and bizarrely quiet. San Francisco was a town of never-ending activity from the trucks rumbling along narrow streets, motorcyclists weaving in and out of traffic and the ever-present stream of people walking, jogging and yakking into cell phones. Now it was still, save for the few attended shops where people were helping each other to nail plywood over the broken windows and sweep up piles of shattered glass.

"Morning," a voice called, making her jump. Jerry was still sitting in the lawn chair, the shotgun perched in the crook of his arm and the finished yellow scarf neatly folded. Wally sat contentedly at his feet, dozing. "Did you get any shut-eye?"

"Not really. Did you?"

He winked. "Sleeping on guard duty? Not likely.

I'm going to find some breakfast for us. If you're looking for your boyfriend, he's gone on a ramble."

Her face flushed. "He's not my boyfriend. I just met him when he was serving in Afghanistan."

Jerry pulled at his mustache. "That's the kind of place that really shows a man for what he is, isn't it?"

She didn't know how to answer. Afghanistan had showed Trey to be duty-driven, stubborn, angry. She realized with a start, it had revealed exactly the same thing about herself with one more trait mixed in…weakness. She'd thought she was strong enough to take anything the war could dish out. How wrong she'd been. How tragically wrong. She realized Jerry was looking at her.

"Where did Trey go?"

Jerry pointed with the shotgun toward the rear of the Imperial. "There. About ten minutes ago."

"Thanks." Sage hurried across the street, trying her best to avoid the pockets of crushed brick and glass as she skirted the enormous crack in the asphalt that was now filling with water, probably due to broken pipes. How would all of it ever be repaired? Crews were still working on the new span of the Bay Bridge after Loma Prieta caused a deck to fail in 1989. It would be months, years even before the city could mend from this massive quake.

She caught sight of Trey and Derick near a mountain of fallen brick and hurried to catch up.

Derick smiled at her, but his eyes were shadowed by dark smudges.

"Rough night in the truck?" she said.

He sighed. "I'm used to better accommodations, but iron man here did fine."

"I've slept in worse places." Trey looked at Sage and she wondered just how dreadful she appeared at that moment.

"Nice sweatshirt. Didn't know you were a Giants fan."

"I'm not, but I can tell you all about the Dodgers. My dad and I used to catch every game we could." She was glad to see his smile. "Shirlene loaned the sweatshirt to me. What are you two looking at?"

"Somewhere under there," Trey said, pointing to the pile of bricks that leaned against the building, "is the stage door. It would be the fastest way to get in, but that option isn't going to play."

Sage bit back a groan.

"So we wait to go through the front door when the police come back and hope the lobby hasn't collapsed," Derick said.

"We could…" she said, then paused to swallow a shiver. "We could go back in through the grate, the way we got out."

Trey shook his head. "I checked that. The building has settled and there is no opening anymore. It's pancaked."

She huffed. "So we just sit and wait and hope?"

Derick looked uncertain. "I guess."

Sage watched Trey closely as his eyes flicked along the brick pile toward the back of the alley. "What? Do you have another idea?"

He scrubbed a hand through his crew cut and Sage found herself amazed that he looked just as perfect as he had in the theater. The dust and the scratch on his cheek did not seem to take the slightest edge off his attractiveness. She knew it was a different story for herself. Her hair was disheveled and dirty and the sweatshirt enveloped her in a cloud of black fleece.

Pay attention, why don't you? She blinked.

"Mr. Long, may I borrow your phone?" Trey said.

"It's Derick," he said, handing it over. "Don't know who you'll be able to get hold of, but have at it. I've been going crazy texting Antonia and my wife, but no response from either one."

Trey squinted at the tiny buttons and Sage tried not to smile as he tapped the keys, his big fingers not cooperating until he finally managed to send a message.

"Who are you texting?"

"My brother. I don't know if he was able to make it back. He knows some people who handle search-and-rescue dogs."

"That would be awesome to watch. Do you think he'll be able to get here?" Derick's eyes were hopeful.

"If he receives the message, he'll get here," Trey said.

If Trey's brother had a small part of Trey's ferocious determination, he'd make it. Sage felt only a measure of comfort. Help could come too late for Antonia. And maybe for Barbara.

They heard someone yell from the direction of the deli, so they made their way back through the maze of debris and found Shirlene and Jerry speaking with two men, one of whom was Sergeant Rubio. He stood next to a man in black coveralls wearing an orange vest. Her heart sped up. Finally, help had arrived.

Rubio divided his attention between Jerry and his receiver. "Okay. We can take an initial look around, but until we get a dog here, it's a cursory search only."

Sage opened her mouth to protest, but Rubio silenced her with a look. "This is Dan Little. He's a volunteer firefighter." His voice hardened. "He's got five kids of his own and I'm not going to risk his life on a what-if. Cursory search only and if things start to come down, we're out. Got me?"

The group nodded and Rubio and Little headed for the front entrance of the opera house, followed by Trey, Sage and Rosalind. Jerry and Shirlene came, too, Shirlene clutching Wally, who squirmed in her grasp.

After another stern warning from Rubio to stay

out of the way, he removed the tape from the doors and stepped over the threshold, flashlight beaming into the darkness.

Sage could see only piles of plaster and some wood paneling that had fallen. She wanted to shout directions at the searchers and opened her mouth to holler in, but Trey shook his head. "They've got to listen."

She bit her lip and stayed quiet.

Five minutes had passed and Sage was now pacing in opposite arcs from Rosalind, who also seemed unable to keep still.

"How long...?" Her words were drowned out by a massive blast that made them all cover their faces. Billows of dust and smoke rose into the air.

Sage coughed and spun toward the Imperial.

EIGHT

"Not there," Trey said, stopping her. "It came from that way."

They looked in horror across the street, behind Jerry's deli at the six-story office building as smoke began to drift through the fractured windows.

Rubio and Little raced out of the opera house and stood for a moment, mesmerized. Rubio's radio crackled to life and though Trey could not make out the words, he read the tension in the dispatcher's voice. Even before Rubio said the words, Trey knew what was coming.

"I'm sorry. We've got to go. We'll be back when we can." He charged away, Little right beside him.

Trey made no move to stop him and neither did Sage. She must have seen the futility of arguing and he hoped she understood. During a disaster you had to look at the big picture. That's why he hadn't been able to stop when Luis went down. He'd had men—and a woman—to protect, and he'd needed to let the medic do his job and handle things. He'd tried to tell her that later, but she hadn't wanted to listen. His mind drifted along with the wisps of smoke that showed clearer now as the sun lightened the sky.

The sound of sirens cut through his thoughts.

"Wait," he heard Derick say. He snapped out of his reverie in time to see Sage stepping into the lobby, Derick trying to grab at her elbow to stop her.

She shook him off and disappeared inside.

Derick gaped. "That's insane. Shouldn't she at least have a hard hat or something?"

Hard hat for a hard head. Trey scrambled inside to catch up. "Sage, this is dumb and you know it. You won't help anyone plowing in here and getting hurt."

He wasn't sure she'd even heard him as she pulled out a flashlight from her pocket and waved it around what used to be the lobby. Now the walls were crumbled, and the mural Antonia had sketched out was missing great chunks of brick from the carefully drawn design. She moved farther in and he strained his ears to listen for the sound of further collapse. Debris grated and crackled under their feet. Wally barked from outside.

The light revealed the archway where guests would step into the theater. Sage made a choking sound. The passage was completely collapsed, impassable without the help of some sort of machinery.

"We can't get in," she said.

"Not that way."

"The back entrance is blocked as well." She looked at him, eyes enormous. "We can't get in and Antonia can't get out."

He searched for something to say. "We don't know that anybody's in there anyway, Sage. Let's go outside and talk about it."

She didn't answer, but neither did she refuse as he led the way back out.

Rosalind and Derick were waiting. "What did you see?" Rosalind demanded. "How bad is it?"

"Pretty bad," Trey confirmed. "It's impassable."

Derick sighed. "Well, I'm half-relieved."

"How can you say that?" Sage snapped. "There might be people in there."

He held up a placating hand. "It's highly unlikely. Antonia is too smart to stay in a collapsing opera house and we're certain Fred left."

"If she was trapped she wouldn't have a choice, now, would she, Derick?" Rosalind raised an eyebrow. "Have you been able to reach her to confirm your theory?"

"No," he said, "but the phones aren't working now. In a few hours, service will be restored and I'm sure we'll get a call from her. I…"

The ground trembled under their feet. Chunks of the ornate cornice pieces tumbled to the sidewalk as they ran for cover.

"Move farther away from the building," Trey called, herding them all back across the street. By the time they reached the deli, the shaking had stopped.

"Whew," Shirlene said, stroking Wally, who had begun to tremble. "Just a small one. It's okay."

They stood on the sidewalk. The sun rose behind the Imperial, ghostly against a fog-draped sky. Shirlene kept a tight hold on Wally, and she and Jerry headed into the deli. "We could all use some coffee, and Jerry's got a camp stove," she called. "I don't want to be alone in my empty store with all this shaking. Creeps me out."

Derick pulled out his cell phone. "Maybe I can get a signal if I head up the street. Be right back." He stopped and clasped Sage's shoulder. "We'll find out she's okay. You'll see I'm right." He beamed her a practiced smile and walked away with Rosalind following, checking her own phone for a signal.

Sage flopped into a chair in front of the deli and Trey pulled up one next to her.

He waited patiently for her to say what was on her mind. It didn't take long.

"This is torture. How can we just sit here waiting for coffee when there is a life at stake?"

"Doesn't appear we have any options at this point." His eyes wandered back to the building behind the Imperial, and he found his mind running through possible scenarios which he did not dare share with Sage.

Jerry and Shirlene brought coffee in disposable cups, and thick slices of bread with butter and blueberry jam. Derick and Rosalind returned, grim-faced.

"We got a signal for a moment, but then it died away."

Sage pulled out her own phone and checked it, too. The device indicated there was a signal, but when she tried to call, nothing happened.

"Lines are jammed," Trey said. "There are 800,000 people in this city and they're all trying to call their families. You just have to wait."

Sage sniffed. "I'm no good at waiting."

He found himself smiling. "I know."

She shot him a hostile look that faded into a sheepish grin that she hid behind her coffee cup.

"We did find out one thing," Rosalind said, swallowing a mouthful of bread. "The apartment building explosion is taking up all the resources at the moment, so the streets are going to remain blocked, at least until nightfall."

"Looks like we'll all be camping out here for a while," Derick said. His tone was cheerful, but Trey thought his expression was less so.

Rosalind shook her head. "I'm getting antsy. I have half a mind to try to get home on foot."

Derick grinned at her. "You want to be a real-life action star. Trust me, it's a lot harder than it is on TV. There are no retakes."

Rosalind sighed. "If we don't hear something soon, I'm going."

"My hero," Derick said, his tone gently mocking.

Rosalind's eyes narrowed. "There doesn't seem to be anything more we can do here. We don't even know if there is anyone inside the Imperial, anyway."

Sage jerked and pulled her phone from her pocket. Trey saw her face go dead white as she clutched it.

"Yes, we do," she said, voice so low he almost missed it.

Trey came close to her. "What is it?"

"I got a text." They crowded around and she turned the tiny screen to face them, holding it with both hands to still the trembling.

Alive. Opra hse. Hlp me. A.

Shocked silence fell over the group until Sage turned the phone around again and texted back. They stared at the tiny device, waiting for a return text.

There was none.

The minutes passed in agonizing slowness, but there was still no reply.

"She's alive," Sage said. "Antonia is alive inside the Imperial."

"How can we get her out?" Derick said, eyes wide. "What can we do?"

Again Trey's gaze traveled to the building behind the opera house. Sage grabbed his hand, her fingers ice-cold.

"You know a way, don't you?"

He wished for once that Sage Harrington could not delve into his thoughts quite so easily.

Sage leapt to her feet. "You know a way in. Tell me right now."

Trey folded his arms across his chest. "It's an idea, that's all. There are a million reasons why it isn't going to pan out, so don't get excited."

She wasn't listening to his cautions. The morning sun picked up the hope gleaming in her blue eyes. He found himself unable to look away, and when she reached for his arms he felt a tightening in his stomach as she held him there, imprisoned in her azure gaze. If she'd commanded, he could have resisted entirely. Instead, she entreated, her voice soft.

"Please tell me what you're thinking, Trey. Please."

He couched his words carefully, hoping she would not remove her hands from his body. "When we were underneath the stage, the other corridor, the one we didn't take, was stacked with some boxes labeled Lamplighter. That's the name of the hotel that's right behind the theater, so…"

"So you think they could share a corridor? There might be a way to get into the Imperial from the Lamplighter?"

He wanted to shut down the tingling that her fingers awakened in his biceps. "As I said, it's plenty iffy."

She moved closer, her warmth taking the chill away from the morning. "It's the best chance we have right now. Let's go look."

He pulled away now. "That's right, we *look*. We assess and weigh the risks."

She grinned and his stomach went sideways again. "Recon only. Got it."

Sage tried to keep from outpacing the others as they made their way past the ruins to the stone facade of the Lamplighter Hotel. The exterior showed signs of damage. The windows were boarded up and the doors secured. Jerry and Shirlene had returned to the deli and taken Wally with them, uneasy at leaving their own stores unattended.

Trey banged on the front door and received no answer. They headed around the back, into a parking area empty except for a Dumpster and a stack of wooden pallets.

Derick shouted and retreated a few steps as a small man wielding a baseball bat leaped out from behind the Dumpster. His bald head was damp, and the armpits of his Lamplighter T-shirt were sweat-soaked. Sage's heart rocked in her chest, but Trey edged forward, both hands spread in front of him, posture relaxed. "Hey, man. Sorry to scare you. We're not here for trouble."

The man gripped the bat. He spoke in Spanish-accented English. "Who are you?"

Trey introduced them all and Sage added, "We think our friend is trapped in the Imperial and we wondered if we could get inside through the Lamplighter."

The man was still not totally convinced, but he lowered the bat to his shoulder. "Emiliano," he said by way of greeting. "I'm the manager. My uncle owns the hotel. I thought you were here to loot the place."

"No, sir," Sage said. "Please, can you tell us if there is a passageway from this hotel to the Imperial?"

He rubbed at a scrape on his chin. "We don't publicize things like that. There's always kids snooping around looking to cause trouble and they can't resist a tunnel. It's like moths to flame."

"So there is one?" she said.

He looked them all over one more time. "I didn't say that." He peered at Derick. "You look familiar."

Derick gave him a brilliant smile. "I'm Derick Long. Are you a movie lover? I've been in a few."

Emiliano's eyes widened. "Yes. You're that actor.

I saw your last movie. It was about five years ago. The one where you were exploring the volcano, looking for some jewel or something."

"The Pearl of Enlightenment," Rosalind interjected. Sage didn't know how she could say the phrase with a straight face, but she seemed as impressed as Emiliano. She caught a slight eye roll from Trey that indicated he felt the same as she did about Derick's cheesy movie.

"You played the part of..." Emiliano snapped his fingers. "Sly Steel. I can't believe it's you. Wait until my wife hears about this."

Sage watched in amusement as Emiliano's countenance changed from wary to wondrous and he gushed on and on until she could stand it no longer. "Please, Emiliano. We've got to get to our friend. She may be hurt. Is there a passageway or isn't there?"

He didn't take his eyes off Derick as he answered, "Yes, there is a passageway. I will show you."

Sage followed Rosalind and Derick and the chattering Emiliano into the Lamplighter Hotel. "What just happened here?" she whispered to Trey.

Trey chuckled. "I believe Sly Steel worked his charm on Emiliano."

Sage grunted. "That movie was terrible."

"I'm with you on that, but it's a good thing Emiliano doesn't agree with us."

The interior of the Lamplighter was relatively undamaged as far as she could see, except for some broken windows, a fallen picture or two and a pile of upended books tumbled from the oak shelves. The lobby was cozy, furnished in dark woods and a variety of green pillows and draperies. A stone-faced fireplace would have made a cozy gathering place in the lobby when the hotel was filled with people.

"Did you have any injuries?" she called to Emiliano. "Any guests hurt in the earthquake?"

Emiliano retrieved some flashlights from a box on the front desk. "No. There were only two couples staying here last night and they left immediately, though I can't imagine how they got out of the city. They said California was no place for them." He turned on the flashlights to check them and handed Derick one almost reverently.

"When is your next movie, Mr. Long?"

Derick shrugged a shoulder. "I've got many projects that I'm considering."

Sage thought he'd spent quite a lot of time considering, since his movie hiatus was going on five years now.

"Why didn't you evacuate?" Emiliano asked.

Derick chuckled. "It's a question I asked myself last night when I slept in a truck that smelled like a sub sandwich. I had to make sure all my employees were out of the Imperial."

Sage thought the line sounded like it might have come straight from Sly Steel's mouth, but she refrained from comment. They filed silently past a well-appointed guest room with the unmade bed indicating a hasty departure. At the end of a hallway, a door opened into a tiny closet with a trapdoor in the floor which Emiliano unbarred and heaved open. The wood gave a spine-tingling squeal as it gaped to reveal a ladder disappearing into the darkness.

Trey edged past Sage and started down. "I'm just going to take a look. Stay here."

"At the end of the passage is a door that leads to under the Imperial," Emiliano called. Sage immediately started down after Trey.

Fifteen rungs took her into inky darkness until her feet splashed into shallow water, soaking right through her shoes and the cuff of her pants.

Trey did not seem surprised to find her there in spite of his direction.

"Looks structurally sound," he said.

Her breath came rapidly as the darkness covered her like a cloak. Nerves prickled all over her body and she was not sure if it was excitement or the remembered terror of their earlier entrapment.

She forced herself forward and splashed by him. "Come on."

He took her arm. "No way. We need to make

plans and carry some supplies. I think you should stay with Rosalind and Derick, and I'll go."

She yanked away. "I'm going. Right now."

His face hardened. "No, you're not. I told you. If we're going in, we're going to be as prepared as we can be."

"You're not the boss here," she said.

"I should be because you're too hotheaded to listen to reason and that makes you a liability to yourself and others."

"It's my life," she hissed and moved around him.

"Really?" he called, voice strange in the small space. "Is that why you're charging off, to prove you're in control of your life?"

"I am in control."

"But that's not why you're doing this."

She didn't turn, afraid of what his next words would be. "I'm here for Antonia."

"No," he said quietly, "you're here to save someone, to make up for Luis and what happened back in Afghanistan because you believe it's your fault he's dead."

She blinked hard, eyes seeing nothing but the blackness that lay ahead. "Maybe it's just as much your fault. You were in charge of security, Captain Black." Sarcasm rang through the air and bounced off the grimy bricks and back to her. "You should have seen it coming and taken action, but you didn't."

He was quiet for a moment. "Yes. I shoulder that blame willingly and I've asked God to forgive me."

"And has He? Has He forgiven you?"

"Yes, I believe so."

"And Luis's family?" Her voice broke, but she forced the rest out. "Have they forgiven you?"

"Probably not."

His tone wasn't bitter, and she splashed forward a few more steps, desperate to get away from Trey before he cut in again.

"You're here," he said loudly, "because you think by saving Antonia and Barbara all by yourself you can ease the load of guilt off your heart, but you know what? You can't. It doesn't work like that, and I can tell you from experience."

"You're wrong," she said. "That's not why I'm down here."

"I've been wrong plenty in my life," Trey said. "But this time, I think I'm dead-on right."

NINE

Trey watched her turn around, and her face was so full of fury and misery that his heart broke. She wasn't a soldier. She was one small woman who held an enormous portion of grief and guilt and, yes, she'd caused some of it herself, but hadn't everyone? Wasn't the point that forgiveness was to be extended because Trey had received it himself when he certainly didn't deserve it? *Forgive me, Lord.* He moved a step toward her.

From somewhere up above came the sound of breaking glass and a shout. Trey ran to the ladder and called up. "What's going on?"

Rosalind shouted down, "Looters. We're in trouble."

Trey charged up the rungs and went full speed ahead until he emerged in the hallway of the Lamplighter where he found Rosalind, eyes wide, holding a bronze statuette like a club. She pointed to the lobby. "They broke in through the side door and Emiliano is trying to fend them off."

"Go down there and tell Sage to stay put." Trey wished he had his M16. One warning volley from that weapon and they'd scatter like scared cats. Then again, the looters might be equally well armed. He took no more time to consider, sprinting into the lobby.

There were three guys, two skinny and white, one heavyset and dark-complexioned. The two skinnies had knives and crouched in a ready stance opposite Emiliano, who held a chair in front of him as if he were a lion tamer. Derick had his fists up, facing the heavyset man.

"Get out," Emiliano shouted. "You won't rob this hotel."

"We'll take what we want," one of them said. He lunged forward as Emiliano swung the chair, which caught him in the stomach. The second one dived toward Emiliano to assist his buddy, but Trey got to him first, grabbing a handful of the looter's long hair and yanking him backward.

He jerked around and Trey and the guy were face-to-face. Trey put him at somewhere in his early twenties, strong under his T-shirt and sagged jeans.

"Listen, kid," he said. "Do yourself a favor and get out of here."

The kid smiled, revealing a chipped tooth. He waved the knife in a smooth arc. "I'll do what I want and you got nothing to say about it."

"You're making a mistake."

"Time for you to die," he said, still smiling, before he lunged at Trey.

Trey did not have to think through the move; it was ingrained in him through many grueling hours of hand-to-hand combat training. He applied both hands at once, the blow on the inside of his attacker's wrist to force his fingers open and Trey's strike to the outside of his hand finished the job, providing enough force to send the knife clattering to the floor.

He let the kid's own momentum take him to the ground before he trapped his hands behind him and used his body weight to pin him to the floor. Adrenaline surged through his nerve pathways, something he had not felt since he'd left Afghanistan. He fought to control it. "You know what?" he could not resist from whispering in the kid's ear. "I think your watch is fast. It's not my time to die after all."

Trey saw that Emiliano's attacker was lying on the floor, unconscious with bits of broken chair scattered around him. The manager raced over with a roll of duct tape to secure the kid who was writhing under Trey's grip. "You hurt?" Trey asked him.

"Nah, but we just had that chair reupholstered. Lousy lowlife," Emiliano grunted as he circled the thug's wrists and ankles with tape. When the stream of profanities issued from the kid's mouth,

Emiliano slapped a piece of tape over his lips. "Save it for the police, boy."

Trey got to his feet. "Where's Derick?"

Emiliano wiped the sweat from his forehead and scanned the lobby. "He must have gone after the big guy."

With a sinking feeling in his stomach, Trey ran along the hallway, checking room after room. He stopped just outside the last bedroom door, his attention caught by a faint sound, someone breathing hard but trying not to. He considered. The breather was tucked behind the bedroom door, waiting for him to step through. Judging by the height and the bulkiness of the person squashed behind the wood panel, it wasn't Derick. He made his choice and prayed he was right, as he kicked out with all his strength at the door. It rocketed back and he heard a grunt of pain as wood contacted skull. It wasn't hard enough to knock him out, just to stun him so Trey was able to grab him from behind the door and put him in a headlock.

Emiliano arrived again with his roll of duct tape, and soon looter number three was secured and marched off to the lobby to await the police.

Trey found Derick a moment later. He was lying on the floor between two twin beds, his nose bloody. Trey tapped his shoulder gently. "Hey, Derick. Can you hear me?"

Derick groaned and opened his eyes just as Rosalind hurried in. She sucked in a breath and dropped to her knees. "Is he hurt badly?"

Trey waited until Derick's eyes focused. "What happened?"

Derick's eyelids fluttered closed again as Rosalind dabbed at the blood from his nose with a tissue. "I tried to stop the guy, but he clocked me."

Rosalind sighed. "When will you learn you're not an action hero, either?"

He offered a shaky grin. "What do you mean? I'm Sly Steel."

She patted his cheek. "Only in the movies, hon. In real life, you're just an actor, a charming, impulsive, regular guy who makes his living pretending."

Derick sat up carefully with a helping hand from Rosalind and Trey. "Maybe I should start playing army captain roles." He eyed Trey. "Seems like you did just fine."

Trey shrugged. "I just work it out as I go."

A gleam of resentment shone in Derick's eyes, which Trey found natural. No man wanted to be found inadequate, especially in front of a woman. "I think you slowed him down anyway. We've got all three in duct tape custody, so to speak."

Derick stood and took the tissue from Rosalind, who continued to try to administer first aid. He shooed her away. "Excellent. Let's get back to work, then. What did you find in the tunnel?"

"Couple inches of water, but it's passable. We'll load up on supplies and go in."

"All of us?" Rosalind said.

"No, we'll leave a team outside to wait for the police and my brother when he shows up."

"Derick, you should stay here," Rosalind said firmly. "You're hurt."

He shook his head. "No way. I'm going in there to help."

Her brows drew together. "That leaves Emiliano to wait for the cops, then, because I'm coming, too."

"We have to leave someone to help him keep watch," Trey said. "Especially since he's got three more to babysit."

Rosalind chewed her lip. "I'll go find someone from the police and make a pest of myself until they come here to collect the looters. Then Derick and I will follow you down. How's that?"

Trey wasn't thrilled, but he couldn't think of a better idea. "Okay."

Derick shook off any gestures of help and they made their way back to the lobby. Emiliano listened as Rosalind rattled off the plan. He nodded.

"That's just fine. I'll be happy to get these punks off my hands." He shot a look at Derick and the blood staining the collar of his shirt. "Are you okay, Mr. Long?"

Derick waved him off. "Just fine. Do you have any supplies we can borrow?"

Emiliano nodded and left the supervising to Derick while he retrieved several flashlights, bottles of water, peanut butter and bread. Trey and Rosalind hastily put together piles of sandwiches, which they distributed between Trey's pack and a small bag he'd found for Rosalind and Derick to carry as well as a handheld two-way radio for each. Emiliano added two pairs of socks to each pack.

He grinned sheepishly. "Socks left in the hotel dryer. Sorry they don't match."

"No worries," Trey said. "It's the best thing in the world sometimes, just to have dry socks. What made you think of it?"

"Spent some time backpacking in South America. Endured my fill of cold, wet feet." Emiliano zipped the packs closed.

Trey and Derick tested the radios.

"Not sure if they'll work down in the tunnels, but it's worth a try," Trey said.

Emiliano nodded. "All set." He looked around. "Is the lady waiting for you in the tunnel?"

"I went down the ladder to tell her to stay put," Rosalind said.

Derick raised a quizzical eyebrow. "Sage doesn't seem like the waiting around type. I'm surprised she didn't come up here to get in on the action."

Trey felt a stab of alarm. "Me, too."

They exchanged a look that made his gut tighten. He grabbed his pack. "I'm going down there. Get the police here as fast as you can. With any luck we'll have located Antonia by then."

Rosalind was already heading for the door as Trey jogged to the room with the trapdoor.

"Be careful," Derick called after him. "Remember you aren't an action hero, either."

Don't I know it. Action heroes likely didn't have their stomachs in knots like he did, wondering whether he would find Sage waiting for him. He agreed with Derick. It was unlike her to sit patiently, but then again, she was not herself, or not the person he'd known before Luis's death, anyway. He was already yelling into the darkness when his feet were only halfway down the ladder.

"Sage? Are you there?"

He continued to descend as he yelled the second time. No answer. The tension in his stomach grew as he hit the bottom, water once again enveloping his boots.

"Sage?" he called once more. His own voice mocked him with an echo as he looked down the empty corridor.

Sage ground her teeth closed to keep them from chattering. She was cold, outside and in. Trey's words cycled through her memory in an unending loop.

You're here because you think by saving Antonia and Barbara all by yourself you can ease the load of guilt off your heart, but you know what? You can't. It doesn't work like that....

He was infuriating and wrong. She was here for Barbara. For Antonia.

She held the flashlight up and splashed around a pile of what appeared to be sodden linens that had spilled from a crate. But if he was wrong, why had she continued on into the darkness, all by herself, with no supplies and no clear direction?

"Because I'm lost," she shouted, kicking at a clump of wet sheet and hearing her words bounce through the darkness. *And I've been lost since Afghanistan.* No longer was her career the all-important driving force. It was not family that anchored her, or faith. She was adrift, so much so that she could not even be sure of who she was anymore. The only thing left was a tiny shred of strength that propelled her. Maybe not forward, but the simple act of being in motion kept the terrible fear at bay.

Trey could not understand that.

She sloshed along, trying to ignore the smell of mildew and the cracks that ribboned the brickwork. The tunnel walls were old, weakened by time and the earthquake. A chip of ceiling fell into the water, flinging a cold drop onto her cheek. She wiped it away with the back of her hand. Ahead a section of the wall had collapsed and a cascade of tumbled bricks filled nearly a quarter of the passageway.

A set of eyes gleamed from the top of the pile as

a rat regarded her curiously. She should have been disgusted, but it was oddly comforting to have another living creature sharing the space with her.

"I'm not going to bother you," she told the rat. "Just here to find a woman. Have you seen one?"

The rat twitched his whiskers and turned away, disappearing back into the yawning darkness. She trained the flashlight toward the place where he had retreated. Cool air blew in from the gap. On impulse she turned the flashlight around and rapped on part of the wall that was intact.

Let there be an answer.

She rapped a few more times just to be sure there was no reply before she edged around the bricks and continued on. The corridor ended abruptly at a closed door, hanging crookedly on its hinges. She pushed at it and it swung open a few inches until it hit an obstruction on the other side. The gap was only about four inches wide. Shoving her flashlight in the crack, she could not see much, but one item made her heart leap. It was an old piece of lighting equipment, twisted and rusted from many years of disuse.

Bingo. She'd found her way into one of the many theater storage areas, which she estimated was somewhere under the stage.

She kicked at the door, startled when a shower of grit trickled down on her from above. "Antonia," she shouted into the gap. "Are you in there?"

Bracing her back against the jamb, she propped her feet on the metal door and pushed with all her might, yielding only a fraction of an inch for all of her effort.

"Antonia?" she yelled louder. A spider scuttled down the wall and she drew back.

She pulled out her phone and texted Antonia again.

Where r u?

Her breath caught when the phone came to life with a reply.

In…

She waited with bated breath for the rest. Nothing else materialized. Sage chewed her lip and pushed again at the door, but she did not have the strength to move it any more. *Use your head, Sage.* She looked around for something to use as leverage.

She retraced her steps down the corridor, scanning the debris on the floor for some bit of pipe or broken board that might be useful. She made it back to the pile of bricks without finding a thing. Once again she beamed the light over the heap, but this time she noticed an area just to the side of the pile that was clear of debris. It gleamed like a dark black eye against the brickwork. Gingerly, she climbed up until she reached the spot, which was about the size of a loaf of bread. She pushed away some of the loose bricks and cleared a larger area, knocking at the aged mortar until the opening was big enough to accommodate her.

Sharp fragments pressed into her stomach as she beamed the flashlight into the hole. She could not tell if it opened into the same storage room she'd been trying to access via the door. What was on the other side? Unstable ceiling? Live electrical wires? An impenetrable darkness that would swallow her whole?

Tremors swept through her torso, her breathing sounding loud and raspy in her own ears. Her body tensed in expectation of explosions, of bullets, of death. And after that…what? Luis had firmly believed he would be delivered into the very presence of God. It sustained him at the end and he had squeezed her hand even as he bled to death, comforting her while he lay dying.

Comforting Sage.

The woman who had led him there.

Comforting the woman who had killed him.

Luis said that Jesus forgave all, and how could a human being do any less? She tried to remember her childhood, when she knew God was real and Jesus forgave all just as clearly as she knew the sun would rise in the morning. When had that sweet certainty slipped away?

Battling back the panic that lay so near the surface of her mind, she inched forward, her head almost through the gap. A hand grasped her ankle and she cried out.

Trey stood beneath her, fury painted on his face. "Planning a one-man sortie?"

She tried for a nonchalant shrug. "One-woman sortie. You scared me."

"I'm not even going to waste my breath," he snapped.

She noticed he carried a pack. "Stocked up at the hotel?"

"I packed supplies. You know what supplies are, right? Those things you need during a well-planned rescue attempt?"

She huffed. "All right. I get it. You're angry, but I got a text from Antonia."

His eyes widened. "Where is she?"

"I don't know. It just said 'in' and that was that. I was trying to get through the door, but it's wedged so I moved on to plan B, as you would say."

Trey's posture was still taut with anger as he left her to try and ram through the door. Though his muscles bulged with the effort, his attempts were no more successful than hers. When he rejoined her, he seemed calmer, as if the physical exertion had drained away some of the anger.

"Let's take a look," he said, starting to climb up next to her.

They both stopped as the pile trembled beneath them.

"Earthquake," he barked, flattening himself on the pile and covering her head with his upper body.

A storm of tiny particles rained down on them. Her neck was twisted at such an angle that she could see the water below, swirling and rippling like a river current. The shaking continued, increasing in intensity.

Sage clamped her lips together to keep from crying out as the pile shuddered and slid underneath them.

The trembling stopped suddenly, but an echo of a scream remained in the air.

Trey lifted his head and eased off of her, his eyes wide and questioning. "That scream wasn't from you, was it?"

Sage shook her head slowly, still dizzy. "It came from behind there."

They both turned their attention back toward the opening, listening to the echo of the woman's scream as it died away.

TEN

Trey eased quickly through the hole and offered a hand to Sage, surprised when she actually took it. Her fingers were chilled in his, trembling violently.

"Okay?" he said, trying to squeeze some warmth back into them.

She didn't look at him. "Sure."

When they were through they both began to yell Antonia's name, their shouts echoing and swirling through the chamber. From somewhere below the sound of water grew louder, but Trey could not discern any answering call from Antonia.

"Where are we?" Sage asked, climbing onto a squat wooden box to keep her feet out of the water.

They both shone their flashlights around the darkness.

"In some lower level storage, I think." Trey used the light to point at a metal shaft with a collection of mangled gears sprinkled around it. "It's the bottom of an elevator platform."

Sage could see it now, a network of pipes and

levers that vanished into the upper darkness. "They were used to raise and lower performers so they could appear and disappear." She thought of an opera she'd attended with Barbara when they were barely out of their teens. Tosca, Puccini's tragic heroine, distraught at the death of her beloved Mario, hurled herself out of the castle window to her death. Though the moment was accomplished with nothing more than some clever stagecraft utilizing a platform like the one in front of them now, the effect was startling.

Trey drew her out of the memory. "Stage tricks before the high-tech days."

"It must have been dangerous," Sage mused. "The platforms moved quickly." She peered closer. "Not many safety measures built in."

"So that means," Trey said, craning his neck, "somewhere up there is the stage. Maybe two stories up?"

Sage wasn't looking up. Trey found her gazing at the water instead. "I think it's rising."

He'd been so focused elsewhere he hadn't noticed. Now he realized the water was flooding in from somewhere and the level was indeed creeping up slowly, but steadily. It was well past his ankles. "Pipes must have ruptured. They had to be rusted in the first place." He located a pipe near the ceiling that spilled water down the cement wall and wondered how many gallons per minute were now pouring into the space. "We don't have much time."

"It sounded like the scream came from above," Sage said.

"Only way up is the elevator shaft," Trey said. Not a surprising turn of events. Nothing about the last two days had been easy so far and that didn't bother him, but he wished he could go it alone, without feeling the inexplicable need to make sure Sage didn't get into any more trouble.

That was a useless wish. True to form, she was already climbing down from the box and splashing toward the rickety contraption. Trey pulled the radio from his pocket. "Derick, can you hear me?"

A crackle of static preceded Derick's relieved reply. "Ten-four, Captain Black. You're not clear, but I can hear you. I was worried after that little shaker. What's happening? Where are you exactly? Have you found her?"

He wasn't sure if Derick's last question referred to Sage or Antonia. "We heard a woman's scream." He relayed the route they'd taken.

"We'll be there as soon as we can. Rosalind's gone for the police, but she's not back yet."

"You might not be able to get through if the water rises much higher. Pipes are shot down here." *And adding a couple more people is the last thing we need in this wreck.*

"Not a problem. Rosalind and I are both great

swimmers, and I can hold my breath for nearly a minute."

Superhero Sly Steel was back. Swell. "Right. We'll keep you posted."

"Ten-four. Over and out."

Trey resisted an eye roll as he moved the radio to his pack to keep it above the waterline and waded after Sage. The elevator was a crisscross of rusted pipes. It supported the actual platform, which was suspended some thirty feet above them, probably at stage level. He presumed if he could climb the network of pipes, there would be a way to exit on to the main stage, which was the most likely place from which the scream had come.

Sage had obviously arrived at the same conclusion. As she grasped the first rung of pipe to start the climb, he laid a hand on her arm. The simple touch seemed to send a shock wave through her and she pulled away so quickly she lost her grip on the bar. He caught her easily, cradling her against his chest, surprised again at how petite she felt there in his embrace. In an action that was no more than a reflex, he was sure, she wrapped her arms around his waist. Sparks charged through his body at the feel of her, painting trails of warmth through his belly and up to his heart. He could not resist putting his mouth to the delicate shell of her ear and whispering, "I've got you."

She gave what might have been the saddest sigh

he had ever heard as she pulled away. "Let me guess," she said. "You want to go first."

The words were sarcastic, but there was something in the tone that betrayed uncertainty, vulnerability, longing even. He was not sure how to respond to it, nor was he sure why he wanted to press her again to his chest. She reminded him of the falcons he'd seen trailing through the impossibly blue skies over Afghanistan. Fierce, strong, determined, but at the same time so delicate that one break in a single slender hollow bone would render them flightless. The previous women in his life had not been nearly this complicated…. *Or fascinating,* his mind supplied from some deep recess where good sense did not reside. *Get it together, Black.*

He swallowed the confusing emotions and edged in front of her. "Yep, I should go first. If the platform starts to come down, I'll yell."

"And what do I do if that happens?" she said, starting up after him.

"Make yourself as small as you can against the side."

He heard her sniff, unconvinced. "And what exactly will you do?"

"Pray," he said automatically.

That silenced her. Trey had to admit he'd sent up a bucketload of prayers already since he'd met this maddening woman a year ago in the middle of a war. Falcons could be admired from afar but for some reason that only God could understand, he was once again up-close and personal with Sage Harrington, their lives linked firmly together. The bars were cold and caked with rust under his fingers. Though he was happy to be out of the rapidly pooling water, their current condition was not optimal.

He planted each foot carefully. Sage moved steadily behind him. About three meters up, he shouted again, "Antonia, can you hear me?"

There might have been a faint reply, or it could as easily have been the old metal protesting under the weight of their ascent. He made it another meter before a pipe broke under his hand, sending him off balance. Skidding down the length of the pipe, he managed to catch himself on the crossbeam, wrapping his legs around it like a bear cub clinging to a tree. He heard Sage calling, voice tight and high.

"Trey?"

"It's all right. I'm secure."

Heart pounding, he let out a breath and heard her do the same from below.

"Let's not do that again, shall we?" she said.

He smiled. "Yes, ma'am," he said, climbing back up, ignoring the abrasions on his palms from his slide down the rusted length of metal. The air was cold and the constant sound of dripping water and creaking metal competed with the loud beating of his heart. He and Sage were now a few more meters from the bottom of the platform. To his right was a fairly solid cement wall. To the left was a small passage that appeared to open onto a sub-stage level. It was too dark for him to see much. To Trey's mind the Imperial was a ridiculous rabbit warren of poorly planned architecture, and he intended to share his thoughts with Derick in no uncertain terms. The thing was ripe for the wrecking ball and nothing else.

Then again, Derick already agreed with him on that, judging from his earlier comments. The only reason he had any interest in the opera house was Barbara, who was either in New Mexico vacationing or the victim of foul play, according to Sage. They'd better find Antonia soon and hope she could shed some light on the whole ridiculous mess, if they survived. He felt a slight shudder in the pipes under his feet.

A low rumbling moan reverberated around them, the noise escalating with every passing second. He could feel the kinetic energy shuddering through the pipes, in his fingers and under his feet, increasing until it was a live thing pulsing all around them. Something snapped above his head.

"Is that sound coming from…?" Sage began.

"Incoming" was all he could think to yell, as the elevator platform above them began to fall.

* * *

She didn't have time to reason it out, only to dive in the direction Trey did, left, into yet another dark void. Something metal rubbed across her cheek and she felt an enormous air disturbance as the platform careened past them, thundering back down to the bottom. The boards underneath her bucked and shook as if in the grip of an earthquake, and she held on to the nearest pipe she could fasten her hands around.

The horrible sound and vibration seemed to last for hours though it could not have been more than a minute. With a final boom, the platform hit bottom, sending a billow of fragments and a shower of water back up the chute.

Sage lay still on her back, feeling the sifting of dust on her face but unable to raise her arm to stop it.

She breathed in and out, eyes closed, listening to her lungs trying to keep up, pleading with her mind not to take her back to that war, to the time and place she could not escape no matter how hard she tried. When the darkness became unbearable, she opened her eyes. Trey was sitting next to her, his expression showing that he understood, that he, too, had been rocketed back in time to the battlefield with its explosions and agony and death.

"Sucks you into the past, doesn't it?" he said

softly, forcing out a slow exhale. "But we're here, and we're all right."

She wondered if he said it as much for himself as for her. "Do you...?" She swallowed. "Do you have flashbacks?"

"Some days none at all and others..." He rubbed the grit from his chin. "Other days it seems like I just arrived home."

She squeezed her eyes closed to contain a sudden onslaught of tears, but one escaped anyway, tracing a hot path down her cheek. "I don't think I ever came home at all." She felt the delicate pressure of his fingertip capturing her tear as if it were a precious pearl.

"You did come home, Sage," he said, his face close to hers. "It may take some time for your mind and heart to catch up with your body. I know it's difficult, probably the hardest thing you've ever done."

"Why is it so hard?" she whispered.

"Because part of us stayed behind with the ones who didn't get to go home, a little bit will always be with them because they blessed us and we won't forget that. I wouldn't want to."

Luis. She remembered his smile, his round cheeks pinked from the desert heat, the way he would consume any food offered him as though it was the finest cuisine prepared by a master chef. How could he be gone? How could she have ruthlessly followed her own agenda and gotten him killed, that decent, loving man with a wife and grandkids to come home for? It should have been her. There were no children waiting. No spouse to grieve. Pain squeezed her heart in a vise-like grip until she thought she could not bear it a moment more.

Trey's lips surprised her, soft and warm, against her temple. Her mind demanded that she pull away, that she draw back into the darkest corner of that terrible place, but her heart lost itself in the warmth, the exquisite ministrations of someone who knew exactly what she was and held out comfort to her anyway. She reached out a hand and clasped it for a moment over his and they stayed there, frozen between fear and relief, her grief, it seemed, flowing through the both of them as time stood still.

Then her mind began to chime in. *Shut it all away. Keep the grief locked inside or you'll drown in it.* She forced herself to sit up, relieved and slightly sorry when Trey got to his feet and redirected his intense gaze to their surroundings.

From above there was a faint rectangle of light silhouetting the gap where the platform had been moments before. It revealed that they were in a cramped rectangular space, interrupted with pipes and broken metal brackets. Trey stood slightly bent over to avoid the ceiling. The wood underneath her feet was pocked in some places where rotten boards had given way and droppings indicated the rodent brigade was thriving.

Trey perched on an area where the floor looked solid enough and fished out the radio. There was no answer from Derick, and he stowed it before he made his way gingerly to the shaft, peering below into the darkness. "We could climb back down, but there's a mess at the bottom and the water's probably waist-high now."

Sage pulled herself to her feet, hugging the nearest pole. "Stage floor is up," she said, pointing a finger in the air.

"Up it is," he said, hesitating. "Do you want me to climb up and check around? I'll come back down for you."

As much as she did not want to climb any farther into the unknown, she wanted even less to be left alone in the dark coffinlike space that seemed to groan and sigh around her like a wounded animal. She shook her head as he put on his backpack again and moved toward the pipes.

She matched her footsteps to his, planting them on the boards that appeared to be relatively intact. It was now a much shorter climb up the chute toward the stage floor and mercifully the pipes were sound.

As they ascended, the air felt warmer, fresher even, and it lifted her spirit a fraction. They were, at least for the moment, working their way back to the surface, to the light, and she felt a near-desperate need to free herself from the bowels of that theater. Trey climbed over the edge and turned to give her a hand up and just like that, they found themselves back on the stage where the horrible adventure had started. It was hardly recognizable. Large sections of flooring had given way and what was left was covered by fallen boxes, ruined tapestries and unidentifiable debris.

Sage couldn't hold back a sigh at the final ruin of the Imperial. "Barbara will be devastated." She allowed herself to believe the story for a minute as she pictured her cousin. Barbara was traveling, away from this painful scene. Perhaps it really was the truth.

From somewhere, a breeze was rippling across the stage, fluttering the tattered flats where they had come to rest atop piles of junk. Skittering rodents appeared and disappeared now and again, whiskers twitching.

A woman's cry froze them both in their tracks.

"Up there," Sage said, making for the ladder that led to the catwalk. She beat him this time, climbing as quickly as she was able, heart pounding and palms cold. "We're coming," she yelled, but the exertion sapped away the volume.

Trey was only a few feet below her. She reached the level where a row of lights was attached, though the bulbs were shattered. Just above was the catwalk, painted black and impossible to see clearly.

Stepping onto it, she moved just enough to allow Trey access.

Gripping the rail, she looked down at the dizzying sight of the mangled stage some thirty feet below. The catwalk itself vibrated under her feet and she wondered just how weakened it had been by the massive quake.

They stared upward, listening to the rattle of wind and the faraway dripping of water until they heard the clang of metal striking metal.

"One more level up," Trey said.

Her body refused to listen to the repeated warnings of her mind and she hurried to the end of the catwalk and started up the ladder to the top. When she'd finished the climb she pulled out her flashlight. The uppermost catwalk was nestled just under the roof and opened onto a ledge not three feet across that had been a sort of partial attic until the floor had failed. The broken boards ended abruptly, their twisted edges projecting out into nothing.

Sage flattened herself against the railing of the catwalk well away from the opening and played her light over the catwalk itself. It was relatively free of debris until the far end, which was partially blocked by a section of roof that had collapsed. Shadows flickered and Sage's skin went clammy. Tiny hairs on the back of her neck lifted as she reached out a hand toward the ruin. Someone was there, she knew it, she felt it.

"Antonia?" she whispered.

Something moved quickly from the other side of the pile. She jerked back and collided with Trey.

"What?" he asked in her ear.

A figure appeared, face sickly pale in the half light. Long dark hair, disheveled and matted, face scratched and bruised, eyes wide with fear or pain or both.

"Antonia," Sage cried, reaching out her hands to the woman who looked momentarily dazed. "We're here to get you out."

Antonia jerked suddenly.

"Hold on to me," Sage shouted, throwing herself on the pile thinking the catwalk under Antonia's feet was giving way.

She heard Antonia's gasp as she was pulled from Sage's grasp. Sage and Trey watched in shock as Antonia's body rose through the air, arms clinging to the rope above her head as an unseen hand yanked her away and her scream was swallowed up by the darkness.

ELEVEN

Trey rushed forward. It was like some ridiculous theater trick. Antonia was there one minute and snatched up and away the next toward a hole in the roof, hauled out by a phantom.

Sage stared at Trey in horror, her mouth moving but no words coming out.

"Fire escape at the reverse end of this catwalk." He ran, the metal walkway bouncing under his feet. He did not allow himself to consider the possibility of the ironwork failing. Leaping over a fallen light that blocked his way and skirting past the twists of wire hanging down from the roof, he reached the outer wall. It was jammed shut. He applied the best cure for that problem, three hard and fast kicks. The door finally flew outward, opening onto a tiny fire escape platform that housed a filthy ladder somehow still clinging to the side of the decrepit building.

His boots rang on the rungs as he charged up, Sage gasping for breath behind him. In a moment he was over the brick lip, dropping down onto the rooftop, startling a duo of pigeons that flapped away. He helped Sage over. They surveyed the roof, which had a definite sag in the middle. Metal boxes housing the ventilation systems and electrical panels obscured their view along with a sizable pile of empty pallets.

"She was pulled out from that side," he whispered in her ear. "Stick to the perimeter. It's probably the most structurally sound." She put her hand in his and he swallowed back the feeling it gave him. They crept forward, heading for the far corner.

They heard another woman's cry. Trey let go of Sage's hand and surged forward, vaulting over the electrical box and onto the back of a man holding Antonia by the arms, sending the guy's baseball cap flying. They rolled over twice. The dude was in shape, hard-muscled and recovering quickly from Trey's surprise assault. He landed a blow on the side of Trey's head that sent sparks dancing through his field of vision. The man got to his feet and Trey took the legs from under him, listening in satisfaction as the breath whooshed out of his lungs.

Sage ran to Antonia and put herself between the woman and the two men.

Over the wash of adrenaline, facts fell into place in Trey's brain along with a slow realization as he surveyed the simple rope harness still around Antonia's waist and the gear lying in a neat pile at the corner of the roof. The man he'd just taken down rolled over. With a groan, Trey offered him a hand and he got to his feet, fixing a glare on Trey, flicking the shoulder-length dark hair aside.

"In what part of your pea brain did that seem like a good idea?"

Trey sighed and brushed off his jeans. "I didn't know you were here."

"Hey, you called me," he said, palms up. "I texted you back, but no doubt you didn't have your phone with you because you're still stuck in the dark ages where people send messages via smoke signals."

Sage put an arm around Antonia. "What is going on?" she demanded.

Trey laughed and retrieved the fallen baseball cap. "A Giants fan now, are you?"

"I'm considering signing with them next season."

"That would be odd considering you can't throw accurately enough to hit the broad side of a barn. Sage Harrington, this is my little brother, Dallas." He took a moment to embrace his brother in a sort of pseudo choke hold around the neck that served as their means of physical connection. It was good to feel him close, strong and half-crazy as ever.

Sage's eyebrows zoomed upward as she took in Dallas's muscle shirt with the barest hint of a tattoo showing over the collar, the camo pants, the hair that hung over his black eyes. "*This* is your brother?"

"In the flesh," Trey said with a grin.

"I wouldn't have guessed that," Sage said.

"We get that a lot. Dallas, this is…"

"Sage Harrington," Dallas finished, interest piquing.

"Yes," Trey said, wedging a warning in the word.

"Comrades in arms." Dallas's eyebrow edged up the tiniest bit, and he stared frankly at Sage as if she was the last piece in a puzzle he'd been searching for.

Trey ignored this and knelt next to Antonia. "Are you hurt?"

"Small injuries only," Antonia said.

"She was banged up, dehydrated when I found her coming out of the tunnels," Dallas said. "Couldn't get out of the stage area so we headed up to the roof, but the collapse blocked our exit. I climbed out and lowered some ropes down to get her."

"You climbed out?" Trey said. "How did you manage that?" He waved a hand. "Never mind. I don't want to know." His brother was a free climber, which Trey was pretty sure translated to "human completely devoid of any common sense."

"How did you get in the theater in the first place?" Sage said.

"There's a storm water system south of here, connects to the drainage pipes under the building. It's locked, but I figured dangerous times call for dangerous measures and all that, so I let myself in. I left it open in case we needed reinforcements."

"How…?" Sage began.

"Trust me," Trey said. "You really don't want to know."

Antonia drank from the water bottle Trey offered her. "My phone died and I thought you would not be able to find me. I banged on the wall for a long time while I was down in the tunnels. I thought I heard someone coming, but after a while I gave up hope of rescue until Dallas showed up. Thank you all. I never should have gone into the theater alone."

"Why didn't you wait outside for me?" Sage said, kneeling next to her. "I've been trying to talk to you for days, calling, leaving messages. That's why we were meeting, remember? I have to talk to you about Barbara."

Dallas cocked his head at Trey.

"Sage's cousin. Husband says she's in Santa Fe," Trey explained.

"But she's not, is she?" Sage finished.

Antonia licked her lips, which were dry and parched. "I haven't seen her."

Sage grabbed her wrist. "You know something. Tell me. I saw you take the photo from the house, as if you were going to search for Barbara or maybe ask people if they'd seen her around."

"I don't know anything for sure."

"Then tell me what you suspect."

Antonia rolled the bottle between her hands. "Barbara and Derick were not getting along. There were fights, explosive ones. And then one morning when I came to work, I was told she was gone, yet the day before she had fixed a time with me to discuss the mural."

"Not exactly proof of anything," Dallas said. "Could have changed her mind as women do, no offense."

Antonia looked at her hands. "You're right. I took the picture hoping to show it around to the workers in the neighborhood, the taxi drivers who do most of the airport runs, to see if anyone really could prove that she had gone there...if that's what happened."

"What else?" Sage pressed. "What aren't you telling me?"

"It is probably nothing."

He thought Sage was going to scream, but she let out a controlled exhale. "Please, Antonia. Tell me what you suspect."

"The night before she supposedly left on her trip, I went to the main house to pick up a sketch I'd left behind. Before I got in, Derick arrived. He was just returning from somewhere. He took off his shoes and laid them out on the step. I don't know why, but he looked so suspicious, so nervous, that I waited until he went inside and I checked the shoes. They were covered in dirt and flecks of gold plaster."

Trey frowned. "Gold?"

She nodded. "One interior wall of the Imperial was painted to look like gold bars at one time. It was part of a publicity campaign in the 1930s. The owner tried to convince people there was a hidden vault under the opera house and charged the patrons a dollar to do a little treasure hunting before the opera. Barbara told me about it. Patrons who discovered the gold wall got a free ticket into the opera."

She bit her fingernail. "I began to imagine that Derick had…killed her and hidden her body in the Imperial. While I was trying to decide what to do about the shoes, I heard someone coming and hid. I saw Rosalind come out and look at the shoes for a long time. Then she took them inside and closed the door. I got more and more suspicious so I decided to check around the theater before I met with you, Sage. I headed for the tunnels, but I felt a small quake so I changed my mind and you know what happened from there."

"If you thought my cousin was in danger, why didn't you go to the police?" Sage said.

Antonia held her chin up. "I have reasons for not wanting to do that."

"What reasons?" Dallas asked flatly.

"Reasons that are my concern," Antonia said, her eyes firing a challenge at Dallas.

Dallas looked more amused than annoyed by

Antonia's response. Sage appeared to be anything but amused.

"I sought you out to talk to you about Barbara. You knew I was concerned. There's no good reason you should have kept me in the dark, unless you're lying."

Antonia's mouth crimped into a grim line. "What reason would I have to harm Barbara?"

"I don't know," Sage said quietly. "Why don't you tell me?"

"I don't have to answer to you." Antonia snatched the cotton bandage out of Trey's hand and pressed it to her forehead.

Sage clamped her lips together and sat down on an electrical box to try her cell phone. Dallas walked to the edge of the building and looked down on the ugly panorama below.

Trey joined him. From their vantage point they could see the skyline, clouded by a mixture of fog and drifts of smoke from what seemed like a half dozen different points. The sun was obscured by storm clouds rolling in off the bay. It was past two but darker than it should have been. Eerie silence made him uneasy; it was unnatural to experience San Francisco without the relentless traffic noise. The city had been dealt a knockout punch.

Dallas spoke without looking at him. "Bad scene."

"Thanks for signing on," Trey said.

"You called. I came. It's a brother thing."

Trey let that sink in. There was so much else he should have done for Dallas, so many times he should have intervened to extricate him from the gang life that ensnared him and nearly ended both of their futures. For now, his brother looked every bit as strong as Trey was and they were side by side, like they had been a lifetime ago. He said a silent thank-you to God.

"You believe it?"

Trey blinked back to the present. "About Barbara's disappearance?"

"Yeah."

"Not sure. Sage believes it. She thinks someone is hiding the truth, and now Antonia has been added to the list along with Derick and Rosalind."

Dallas kept his face pointed to the horizon. "And you want to get into that? With her?"

No, he wanted to shout. Yes, no, maybe and everything in between. With Sage, he could not think, only feel, and what he felt scared him to the core. "I have to."

"No, you don't."

He watched three pigeons waddling around the rooftop as if it was a normal day and the city hadn't just fallen to its knees. "She's...struggling with what happened, to Luis and to herself."

He nodded. "And you are, too."

"I guess," he sighed. "But I've got more tools to deal with it."

"You only really need one."

A beam of sunlight made it through the clouds and flickered over the old cement. "She doesn't have faith."

"Then share that with her, but whether she takes it or not is her thing."

"I know."

Dallas nodded. "You know, but you have this inability to quit when you should."

Trey gave him a look. "Family trait. I'm helping her get through this disaster. The rest of the problem she'll tackle her own way."

"Without you."

"Sure."

He shrugged. "All right. So how do you want to play this? You're the big-shot G.I."

There was pain in those words, the deeply buried desire that was never realized by his brother who had wanted nothing in his whole life but to join the military. Trey wondered if he had found a replacement for that burning passion, but it was not the time to ask. "Get the women out of here. Leave the Barbara issue to the police."

Dallas gave him a sideways grin. "And you think Sage is going to say 'yes, sir' and go along with your plan?"

"She's never gone along with a single thing I've said since I met her."

He laughed. "I knew I liked that girl."

When Antonia had recovered somewhat, Sage helped her to stand and they picked their way over to join Dallas and Trey. Trey pulled supplies from his pack and handed around bread with peanut butter and water bottles. Sage looked into his pack. "Do we get a candy bar if we finish our lunches?" She enjoyed the flush that rose to his cheeks.

"I was going to save those for later."

She turned to Dallas. "Was he a candy junkie as a kid?"

Dallas smiled. "The worst kind. Never met a type of candy he didn't like."

"Not true," Trey said, giving them an offended look. "Black jelly beans are horrendous."

"I stand corrected," Sage said, devouring her sandwich quickly. "How do we get out of here and bring back the police?"

Options were bandied about between the four of them. The best choice seemed to be to rappel down the outside of the building to the closest working fire escape. Then they could climb down to the ground one at a time. The plan would prevent them from having to reenter the opera house at all. Antonia looked a little wan at the prospect, but she nodded.

"I'll just be glad to get out of here," she said, wiping away a tiny drop of rain that splatted her cheek.

Sage noticed that Antonia did not meet her eye. More than ever, she was convinced the woman knew something she was not telling. *Fine, if you don't want to talk to me, you're going to tell it to the police.*

Trey radioed Derick, but again there was no answer. He had Dallas try with his cell phone with no better luck so his brother sent a cursory text message to Derick's phone.

Antonia safe. On our way out. Wait for us at deli.

It was the best they could do. Sage hoped that Derick would not go into Sly Steel mode and head inside anyway. A more sinister thought occurred to her. If Derick had imprisoned Barbara, or killed her, he would want everyone to stay as far away from the Imperial as possible. She caught the worry lines etched into Trey's forehead, accentuated by the light rain that had begun to fall, and sidled over to him.

"Not sure about the escape plan?" she asked.

"It's not that." He meticulously straightened the first aid kit. "Remember when we found Wally?"

She shivered. "Yes. He was bloody."

"Uh-huh, but Antonia has only minor cuts and scratches."

A tingle crept up her spine. "So whose blood was on the dog?"

Trey didn't answer, and his silence added to her rising sense of dread. Was it Barbara's blood on Wally? Perhaps Fred Tipley hadn't made it all the way out of the Imperial and he'd gotten injured? And what about the person who'd tried to crush them with boxes? She let herself imagine it for one brief moment, her cousin or Fred, dying alone in the darkness, cold and terrified. The thought coiled through her like a snake, sinking sharp pricks of pain into her heart. She forced herself to breathe. There was simply no time for a panic attack.

Hold on, Barbara. The police will make Derick tell the truth and we'll come and get you. I promise. They made their way to the fire escape, Trey first, then Antonia, Sage and Dallas bringing up the rear.

Antonia was breathing fast as she climbed backward down the rusted metal rungs. "What is it they say? Don't look down?"

"Right," Trey said. "One step at a time."

The ladder creaked under their weight, but Sage did not allow the sound into her consciousness. One step at a time. So far she had taken many steps that would have seemed impossible to her only hours before. The thought gave her a little spurt of courage and she nursed the burgeoning belief that the whole nightmare might actually have a good outcome. Antonia was the proof that would convince the police and prompt a full-scale search. She just had to get back to level ground. One step at a time.

Trey called up to her and she and Dallas stopped to listen.

"Bottom ladder is gone," he yelled.

She had to have heard him wrong.

"Come again?" Dallas shouted.

"The ladder below us has fallen away from the building."

"How far to the ground?" Dallas called.

"Roughly six meters. We'll have to use the ropes."

Trey's radio crackled to life.

"We've finally got a cop here." Derick's voice was too loud.

Trey explained their position. "Coming down now and we've got plenty to discuss with that cop."

Sage couldn't detect any undue concern in Derick's response, but perhaps the static masked it. She looked down on Antonia. Her lips were pressed together, hands clutching the damp fire escape platform. Was her tension caused by the danger of their descent? Or because she feared meeting with the police at the end of the journey?

TWELVE

Trey waited until they had all joined him on the lower fire escape platform. He left the rope management to his brother and busied himself with tying a makeshift harness around his waist for the descent.

"Isn't it women and children first?" Sage said. He caught the fear there, but her attempt to control it with humor was a good sign, he thought.

"Since I outweigh any of you, I ought to be a good test subject."

"If you crash to the ground we'll know the ropes aren't going to support the rest of us?" she said.

"Something like that." He tightened the rope while his brother worked on securing the other end with Antonia's help.

Sage reached out tentatively, her fingers barely touching the skin of his forearm. He froze, staring at the spot. She struggled to speak.

Trey made things easier. "It'll work," he said, flashing a cocky smile.

She kept her hand there, the fingers soft as petals. "It just sort of came to me...."

"What?"

"That this is probably the last thing you would have chosen. Being here, with me." A tenuous band of sunlight broke through the rain clouds and illuminated the shadows of fatigue around her eyes. "After..." She cleared her throat and pulled away. "Never mind."

He leaned closer, his voice barely a whisper. "I'm not angry about what happened anymore, just grieving, like you, like we all are."

"But not blaming yourself." There was a question entwined in her words.

"I'll always wonder what I didn't do, but staying there, in that place, isn't what God wants from me." He bent so he could look straight into her eyes. "Or you." He waved a hand at the mangled city around them. "I guess this earthquake reminded me of that."

"I wish I could bring myself to believe it."

And how he wished he could help her to that place of peace, and what a craving stirred inside him to pull her to him and hold back the memories that fought to bring her down. His heart pounded as she grasped his wrist and quickly brought it to her lips. "Be careful, Captain Black."

Breath raspy, he covered his emotion by finishing his work on the rope. "Yes, ma'am."

He stepped to the edge and gave his brother a thumbs-up.

"Easy, man," Dallas called.

Trey leaned out backward until only his toes touched the metal platform and then he stepped off, legs spread to keep from spiraling. Flakes of rust fell away from the metal, peppering his cheeks, and he was lowered in a series of jerks, though he knew his brother was doing his best to let out the rope slowly. The sidewalk spun below him, the rope cinching uncomfortably around his waist, and rain spattered his clothing. His pulse slowed as he grew closer to the cement, which had buckled in some places, the gutter running with water from broken pipes.

The moment his boots touched down he immediately untied the rope and Dallas reeled it back up through the rain, which had begun to fall in earnest. Derick, Rosalind, Emiliano and Sergeant Rubio arrived just as Sage reached the ground and they sent the rope back up for Antonia.

"You all are not good at following directions," Rubio said with more resignation than ire. "I see you found your missing woman. Good work."

Derick grasped the rope at the bottom, but Trey took it from him. "I've got it," he said, ignoring the actor's irritated hands-on-hips move.

They all craned their necks to the sky to track Antonia's descent. As soon as she reached ground level, Derick wrapped her in a hug. Antonia shoved him away.

"Don't touch me," she hissed.

Rosalind's eyes widened as she looked from Antonia to Derick. "Problem?"

Antonia took several steps back and folded her arms across her chest, eyes riveted to the wet cement.

As curious as he was about Derick's reaction, his attention remained on his brother, who made his way down the rope, lithe as a cat.

"Who's this?" Rosalind said.

Trey made the introductions and explanations as her eyes widened.

"He crawled through the storm drains? I didn't know that was even possible."

Dallas raised his fingers. "Scout's honor."

Rubio wiped the water from his hat. "Let's take this inside somewhere."

Emiliano led the way back to the hotel and insisted they sit in the lobby. There was no electricity, so the room was lit only by the wan daylight and a battery-powered lantern. Emiliano explained with satisfaction in his tone as he passed around warm sodas from the vending machine that the three thugs who'd tried to loot the place had been taken away.

Sergeant Rubio seated himself in a wooden chair, exhaustion written all over him. The guy had been on duty now since the quake hit, Trey figured. No rest for emergency personnel during a catastrophic event. Rubio drained the soda in four gulps.

Trey and Dallas chose to stand. They were eager to see how things played out when the issue of Barbara was out in the open.

Sage didn't waste time. "My cousin Barbara is missing, Sergeant Rubio. I have reason to believe she's been imprisoned in the Imperial."

Derick gaped. "What? By whom?"

"By you," Sage said.

His face went pale, then flushed a rosy pink. "Are you crazy? I love Barbara. She's in New Mexico, like I've told you a hundred times already."

Sage didn't flinch. "I don't think so. Antonia doesn't either."

Derick blinked at Antonia. "What have you been saying?"

"I saw you return from the opera house with your shoes all full of mud and gold plaster just before she supposedly left town," Antonia said.

He made gasping noises as if someone was trying to choke him. "I… Of course I spend time at the opera house. Yes, I was there in the basement, I don't deny it, but not to bury my wife or whatever it is you're trying to insinuate. I was checking, you know, to be sure it was not flooding again."

Rosalind shifted, gaze flicking over Derick and then quickly away.

Sage turned to Rosalind. "You saw the shoes, too. You cleaned them off and brought them inside. Why?"

Rosalind shoved a section of hair from her face. "Because they were dirty. Derick is not accustomed to taking care of himself and since Barbara left town, someone needs to do it. They were dirty shoes, not a smoking gun or bloody gloves."

Derick was shaking his head, face stricken. "I love my wife. I love Barbara. How could you believe that I would do anything to hurt her?"

Trey knew enough to realize that Derick's reaction could be a product of his profession, a well-staged act for their benefit.

"Really?" Antonia said bitterly. "You love her? Then why did you try to seduce me?"

Derick's mouth fell open.

Rosalind stood up. "That's enough. We've just gone through a major catastrophe and now is not the time for opportunism."

"Are you saying I'm lying?" Antonia snapped.

Rosalind's tone sharpened. "I've been working for the Longs for a while now and I know how the game is played. This isn't my first rodeo, honey." She addressed Rubio. "I can't tell you how many celebrity-struck girls have chased after Derick, thinking that they could make him realize they were his true heart's desire and not because they cared about him. They would do anything to get a piece of his fame."

Antonia shot to her feet and Sergeant Rubio held up a calming hand. "Keep it under control," he warned. "Ms. Verde, are you saying that Mr. Long forced his attentions on you and this is why you think he might have killed his wife?"

"I didn't kill anyone," Derick shouted. He looked as though he was going to leap out of his seat, so Trey went behind and applied a hard downward pressure to his shoulder.

"Let the lady talk," Trey growled.

Rubio was distracted by a message coming over his phone.

"That's what I suspected," Antonia said. "And no," she said grudgingly. "He did not violate me, just made it clear he wanted more than painting from me."

"But you are not exactly the pinnacle of virtue are you?" Rosalind stared her down. "You don't think we do background checks on our people? The only reason you were hired is because Barbara wanted to give you a chance."

Antonia's lips thinned into a tight line and she looked at the floor. "My past has nothing to do with this."

"No? You didn't need to score a little cash to help out your sister, who is in jail? Cops thought you helped her commit her crime, didn't they?"

"Don't talk about my sister." Antonia choked the words out.

Derick grasped Rosalind's wrist. "Leave her be. She misunderstood my intentions. Let's just straighten this thing out."

Sage turned to Rubio. "Send in a team. Search the Imperial. I'm telling you my cousin is in there."

Rubio stood up, putting his phone away. "No, she's not. I alerted the desk sergeant that Mr. Long was looking for her after our conversation at the deli. I just got a message. Mrs. Barbara Long called the station three hours ago inquiring about her husband's well-being when she could not reach him on his cell phone. They finally had a moment to message me with the information." He looked regretfully at the empty soda can. "I've got to go. There's no reason to put yourselves at any further risk. Rest up, roads will be partially cleared before too much longer." He turned to Emiliano. "Can they bunk here for a while?"

Emiliano nodded briskly. "Of course."

"Okay, then," Rubio said. "I'm glad this is all over."

Sage decided she should be feeling the swell of relief, or maybe even the tingle of guilt for her earlier accusation, but she was numb. Barbara really was fine. The whole episode had been an invention of her mind, her imagination, her paranoia. Now her cheeks burned. "I…I guess I have an apology to make," she said to Derick. "I'm extremely sorry."

He stood, beaming, and hugged her around the shoulders. "Don't give it another thought. I should be flattered that you think I could be clever enough to make Barbara disappear." He leaned closer. "I really do love her, you know."

She endured the hug for a moment before she stepped back. Antonia hadn't moved, her expression stony.

"Don't you owe Derick an apology, too?" Rosalind said to her.

Sage heard the girl's sharp intake of breath. "I'm not going to apologize to a man who tried to take advantage of me."

"I'm not surprised," Rosalind said. She turned to Emiliano. "Thank you for letting us rest here awhile. Is there somewhere I could lie down?"

Emiliano snapped into host mode. "Certainly. Perhaps a room for you and…" he hesitated, eyeing Antonia. "The other two ladies can share. Gentlemen, we have two other rooms that aren't damaged if you don't mind doubling up."

"My brother and I will split a room," Trey said quickly.

Derick nodded. "That would be better than sleeping in a truck, and I'm told I talk in my sleep so it's just as well I have my own room."

Sage wondered what Derick might mumble while

asleep. Was he the devoted husband? Shocked at the accusations? Or the man who had tried to force himself on Antonia? Rosalind had acted quickly to discredit Antonia, a little too quickly perhaps? Was she guilty of covering something up for Derick? Sage knew she was trying to salvage her own tattered feelings. Derick was innocent of hurting Barbara. The rest didn't matter much.

She followed Antonia to a cramped guest room on the other side of the hallway.

Emiliano pointed the way. "Bathroom is across the hall. Water isn't working, so we'll use the outhouse the construction guys left in the parking lot. At least we can wash with bottled water. I'll leave a gallon next to the sink."

"Thank you, Emiliano," Sage said and Antonia echoed her gratitude. He answered with a smile and a self-deprecating wave before he left.

So many people. Giving so selflessly. It made her burn with shame to think of how she'd spent the last year, so deeply buried in her own problems, blindfolded from the world. Before, she'd been so zealous to help others by exposing the truth, capturing the photo that would change everything. Had it really been about helping others? Or helping her own career? Antonia lay down on the bed, her back to Sage.

They had both convinced themselves that Barbara was the victim of foul play. Antonia's theories were perhaps driven by a secret attraction to Derick, but her own? The rain pounded down on the roof of the little inn, and she pictured Trey, sacrificing his own safety for hers and entertaining her crazy notion that Derick had kidnapped his own wife.

Across the hall she could hear the murmur of voices. She left the room, closing the door behind her, and found Rosalind deep in conversation with Derick in the room Rosalind was occupying. They broke off when they saw her.

Derick's face flushed. "I'm still in shock that you thought I could hurt Barbara," he said with a tremble in his voice.

Sage felt her own cheeks suffuse with blood. "I'm sorry. I think…" she began, then cleared her throat. "I wanted to invent a purpose for myself, and it all seemed to fit together. All I can do is apologize again and ask your forgiveness."

He nodded slowly. "Maybe that's why I'm an actor. I guess it allows me to reinvent who I am, too, into someone stronger and braver and more interesting than the person I actually am."

She saw misery in his eyes as Rosalind put a hand on his shoulder. "You're a good man, Derick," Rosalind said. "That's what gets you into trouble. Women mistake kindness for something else."

"Not Barbara," Derick said softly. "She knows me for exactly who I am and she loves me anyway."

He smiled. "Most of the time, anyway. When she comes home, I'm going to straighten everything out and ask her to forgive me."

"For what?" Sage said before she could stop herself.

Rosalind cut him off. "For all the dumb things he's done and said." She looked closely at Sage. "I'm sure we've all got a list of those. I know I do."

Sage nodded and excused herself, but before she left she could not resist one more question. "You said Antonia was in trouble with the law. What sort of trouble?"

Both Rosalind and Derick looked uncomfortable. "It doesn't seem right to spread it around, but I suppose you should know since you're rooming with her. Her sister is in jail for attempted murder of her husband. Antonia was suspected of helping her, but the police couldn't prove anything."

Sage gaped. "And you hired her anyway?"

Rosalind shot a sideways glance at Derick, who looked at his shoes. "She seemed very earnest when we brought it up, and she had a convincing story. She's also an incredibly talented muralist, so Barbara lobbied hard to have her hired and, well, at the end of the day, the Imperial is Barbara's project." Rosalind sighed. "She started to fawn after Derick, make excuses to be close to him, laugh at all his jokes and flatter him. Starstruck, like most people who have seen his work."

"They don't care about my work," Derick said with an unusual note of bitterness. "I'm famous and they cling to that. Doesn't matter who I am or how good an actor. You're right, Rosalind. They want me because they can grab some of that fame. In another ten years when all the parts dry up, I won't be able to pay them to drink coffee with me."

In the poor light, Derick looked old and disheveled, a tired middle-aged man with dirty clothes and harsh creases slashed across his forehead. Sage wanted to say something then, to comfort him somehow, but she had no idea how to do it. Age was stripping him of his identity, and the war had done that same thing to her.

She closed the door behind her and made her way to the far end of the hallway, to an exit that opened onto a charming courtyard. Under the eaves was a set of chairs, tumbled over from the earthquake, amidst some sturdy potted azaleas that had defied the shaking and stayed upright. It smelled of rain, and the fading daylight showed moss tucked between the stones of a planter that ran the perimeter of the little sanctuary. Heaving one of the chairs back up onto its legs, she sat, eyes closed, and listened to the rain as it pattered down around her.

Wash me clean. An impulse beat strong and silent within her. With the sound of the water ringing in her ears, she found herself on her feet again and stepping out into the storm. Cold droplets cascaded down on her upturned face, running over her neck and arms. *Wash away the past,* she begged, the thought springing from somewhere deep inside. *Cleanse away the grief and guilt and anger and pain and help me find out who I am again.*

Was she talking to God? Did she really have the right?

One of her senses, which somehow still functioned against the wild wanderings of her mind, told her she was not alone. She knew she would open her eyes and find the one person who could possibly understand, the only man who knew her at her worst.

Rain blurred her vision. Blinking, she found it was not Trey who had joined her, but Dallas.

THIRTEEN

Dallas leaned against the doorway to the porch. "Sorry," he said. "I'll beat it."

Sage stepped back under the eaves and wiped the rain from her face. "No, it's okay. I was just…"

He cocked his head. "You don't have to explain it to me."

She gestured for him to join her and he straightened a fallen chair and sat down. They were quiet for a long time, staring into the silvered rain.

"You can almost forget about it all, sitting here," Dallas said, taking off his baseball cap and setting it on the arm of the chair.

The quake? Or the past? She wasn't sure to which he referred. His shoulder-length hair shadowed his face, and she saw a scar snaking from under his shirt and across his collarbone. "You aren't what I expected."

"I'm not what anyone expected, but what in particular do you find surprising?"

"That you're Trey's brother and he's such a…"

"Captain America type?"

She smiled. "I guess."

Dallas raked the hair off his face and laughed. "So you two haven't talked much about his earlier years."

Had they? In those rare quiet moments in Afghanistan, he'd wanted to know about Sage, her family, her training, her interests, but she now realized he'd managed to deflect all of her probing questions. Curiosity burned inside, a long-forgotten sensation. She tried to think of a polite way to pry but gave up. "What happened?" she said simply.

He turned enigmatic black eyes on her. "His story to tell."

"You brought it up."

His grin was wolfish. "True. Bolsters my bad-boy persona, doesn't it?"

She didn't take the bait. "So what happened?"

"Like I said, that's his story, but I can tell you mine, the short version, anyway."

She curled her legs under her on the chair, heedless of the wet fabric of her jeans sticking to her calves. "Tell away."

"You sure I'm not interrupting your rain dance?"

"Stop stalling and spill it."

He laughed again. "I can see why Trey likes you."

Tolerated was more apropos than *liked*. Though her cheeks warmed, she didn't allow herself a smile.

Dallas gazed again at the falling rain. "I'm four years younger than Trey and I wanted to be like him every single day of my life. Baseball, bike riding, rock climbing, whatever it was, I tried to do it just like Trey did."

"Hero worship?"

"Brother worship of the highest order. My mom raised us by herself after my dad died when I was eleven. She loved it that we were always together. 'Take care of each other,' she told us every day as we left for school." His eyes roved the courtyard. "After Dad died, things changed. I was angry that he went that way. He was a truck driver and he fell asleep at the wheel. It was mundane, a prosaic way to die for a retired marine. Dad was invincible and I couldn't understand it."

Sage thought about her own father, how he always smelled of coffee beans, an occupational hazard of owning a little coffee shop with her mother. He'd tried to talk to her, to help shoulder the burden she'd come home with. They all had—her mother, her sister, Erika—but she'd shut them all out, made more and more excuses to be farther and farther away from the people that loved her. Water splashed over the eaves and puddled on the cracked cement. The corners of his mouth tightened. "I started to slide. Looking to be the tough guy, prove myself with the wrong crowd. I was under the spell of a bad influence, flirting with the gang thing. My mom got scared and sent me away to live with my cousin, but it followed me." He tapped his bad leg. "I paid the price for that. Nearly died, and ruined my chance to be a marine like my dad."

Sage wanted to say something comforting, but she did not think he would welcome the sentiment.

"Healed up and straightened out, finally, but Trey still feels guilty."

"Because he didn't steer you away from the bad influences?"

Dallas stared at the trickling water, the growing darkness hiding his expression. "Getting late."

"Is that the end of the story?"

He got to his feet stiffly and stretched his arms over his head. "Enough strolling down that lane of bad memories for now. I'll tell Trey you're out here. He's helping Emiliano cover some broken windows because he doesn't know how to wind down. He'll probably start remodeling the place if Emiliano lets him. Catch you later."

"Why does Trey feel guilty about your choices?"

Dallas gave her something halfway between a frown and a smile. "Like I told you, his story to tell."

He tossed the words over his shoulder, forgetting to take his baseball cap as he left.

Trey finished taping the last window, surveying his work with satisfaction. Something smelled like food and his stomach sent up a growl. He followed his nose to the kitchen and found Sage standing over a one-burner camp stove, stirring a pot of soup. She pointed with the spoon at the hat on the table. "Dallas left his hat on the porch."

Shirlene was with her, slapping together cheese sandwiches. She gave him a friendly salute with a mustard-covered knife.

"Hello, soldier. I heard your platoon rescued the painter gal."

"Yes, ma'am. It was a cooperative effort."

Jerry appeared and immediately handed a trembling Wally into Trey's arms.

"He's driving me crazy, whining, yelping, clawing up my doormat and he even chewed a hole in one of my cupboards. We decided he must miss you so we brought him over. I'm done being Grandpa Jerry. There's a good reason why I never had kids."

Trey laughed, stroking Wally's head. "Troublemaker," he said to the dog, who rewarded him with a lick under the chin. "That soup smells good."

"This from a guy used to eating MREs." Sage smiled but followed up with a look he could not figure out. He wondered how she was feeling about the fact that Barbara was accounted for and the trauma was over. He knew how he felt now that there were no more windows to board up.

Derick and Rosalind were cleaning the debris from a table in the lobby and putting out paper napkins. "Rubio said the road will be clear enough to start letting people out in the morning," Derick called. "Back to civilization."

Trey wondered why he did not share the relief he heard in Derick's tone. Sage didn't meet his gaze but continued to stir as if she was keeping the planets in orbit with each careful rotation of the spoon.

"Where is your brother?" Rosalind asked.

"Gone exploring again." Trey caught the multiple sets of raised eyebrows. "I think he's going to make a return trip via the storm drains after he satisfies himself that there is nothing more for him to do."

"He didn't want to stick around for sandwiches?" Emiliano said.

"He doesn't stay in any one place for too long."

Sage finished her meticulous stirring and spooned up soup into paper bowls while Shirlene carried a plateful of cheese sandwiches to the table. There was not enough room for everyone to sit, so the men stood and juggled their bowls and sandwiches while Sage, Rosalind and Shirlene squeezed into the chairs, leaving one empty for Antonia.

"Antonia was asleep, so I'll save her a sandwich," Sage said. Again he thought he caught a questioning look from her when she spoke to him, but he couldn't figure out what she wanted to know. He gave Wally a quarter of his sandwich.

"I guess we'll bunk here for the night, if that's okay with you," he said to Emiliano.

"Sure," he said. "And you two can sleep on the sofas if you need a place," Emiliano said to Shirlene and Jerry.

"No, thanks," Jerry said, wiping soup from his mustache. "We just came to offload the dog and see if you had anything better to eat than bread and jam. We've got to keep watch at our stores."

Following dinner, Jerry and Shirlene left and the hotel grew dark with only small pools of light from the lanterns.

Trey's muscles began to feel heavy as fatigue finally set in. He wanted to talk to Sage, to get her alone and see how she was dealing with things, but she stuck close to Rosalind and Emiliano. Staying busy? Avoiding him until they parted ways for good this time? An ache settled behind his ribs and stuck there until he finally made his way to the bathroom and washed up as best he could, offering Wally a drink of water from a paper cup. Back in his empty room, he lay down on the bed. Wally leaped up easily and curled himself next to Trey, who stroked the little dog.

"Miss your owner?" He worried that Fred might have been trapped somewhere as he left the theater, maybe injured in a crash. Or worse. After Sage left, if there were no police officers around to help, he would try to find Fred's new apartment and if that failed, he'd search for Fred street by street until he found him.

Stupid, Trey. Was he trying to stay wrapped in a mission? To avoid thinking about never being close to Sage Harrington again? His eyes closed but his mind would not shut off. He tried picturing the wooded acres of land high in the mountains, the place where he intended to build a cabin, board by board, nail by nail, with his own hands. Close to his mother, who refused to leave the little town where she'd raised them, near a seasonal creek where he might be able to entice his brother to come and fish, if Dallas could remain in one spot long enough. A short drive from town where he would set up a carpentry shop. The image had always soothed him, but for some reason it didn't at that moment.

He rolled onto his side, which earned him a disgruntled sniff from Wally. A soft tap sounded at the door.

Sage stood in the doorway, small and waiflike in the soft glow of the lantern she held. She bit her lip. "Were you asleep?"

"No." He fingered the door uncertainly. "Something wrong?"

She shook her head. "No, nothing. I couldn't sleep. I was going to get a drink of water and I figured I'd ask if you wanted anything."

He blinked and tried not to let his eyes round in surprise. "Sure."

He followed her into the lobby, which was empty, and sat on the sofa in the darkness while she rummaged in the kitchen by lantern light, returning with two slices of pie and a bottle of water.

"I thought pie might go well with the water. Emiliano said we might as well eat it since it's getting stale," she said, handing him a fork.

He took an experimental taste. "Pumpkin. My mother makes the best pumpkin pie in the universe, but this is pretty good," he said after another mouthful.

She nodded in agreement. "Not as good as candy, though?"

He laughed. "In an emergency, you've got to make do."

Her giggle touched something inside him, and he desperately did not want to break the thread that bound them together in that moment.

"I talked to Dallas for a while before he left."

He swallowed another bite of pie. "Uh-huh."

"I didn't know you had a rough childhood."

He felt his breath come out in a long sigh. "I'm surprised he shared that."

"He didn't. Not much, anyway. It just made me realize that I never asked you about your life. I was too wrapped up in my own."

"It's not much of a story. I got involved with a

gang. Tried to get out of it. Wound up ensnaring my brother in spite of the fact that Mom moved him."

She gaped. "You were the bad influence on Dallas?"

Even after so many years, the pain coursed through his gut. His mother had had to move Dallas away from his only brother and that shame would never leave him.

"What made you change for good?"

He put down the unfinished pie and cleared his throat. She was asking for the truth and he'd give it to her, though it felt like ripping off a bandage from a fresh wound. "I'd actually thought I'd gotten out, enlisted and was ready to leave for boot camp when Dallas got beat up by a rival gang so badly he nearly died. He lost part of his spleen and some vision in his left eye, messed up his knee. Ended his chances to be a marine." He blew out a breath. "My choices killed his dreams, but fortunately God spared his life."

Her eyes were huge in the lantern's glow. "How did you ever forgive yourself?"

"I asked God to forgive me first."

"And He did?"

"And He did. I've worked to make things right with my brother every day since. We're better and I hope that someday we'll be as close as we used to be."

He thought he saw the sheen of moisture in her

eyes. Slowly, he reached out a tentative hand and clasped her wrist, feeling the rapid beat of her pulse there. Unable to resist, he pressed his cheek to her palm and felt her soft skin caress him. "It's not easy because I'll always remember what I did and so will Dallas."

"Oh, Trey."

He did not want the pity he heard in her voice as he straightened. "It's okay. Forgiveness isn't forgetting, it's just a step toward being the person God wants you to be." Suddenly there was a catch in her breathing and her hand trembled under his. He understood why she was asking about his past.

"I can't forget," she whispered, tears spilling now.

He pulled her close and she snuggled into his embrace, thrilling every nerve in his body. "You won't ever forget, but you can overcome because He gives you the tools and the strength." He pressed his lips to her temple. "He's already done the hard work and saved you, all you have to do is accept it."

He felt his own heartbeat speeding up to match hers, as if their bodies were working together in that moment, entwined in a precious sort of synchronicity. She pressed her face to his chest.

"It's been a horrible week, but..."

"But?"

"I've been starting to feel things, bad things and

frightening ones sometimes, but at least it's something besides just the numbness."

"That's progress. Maybe that's even healing," he ventured.

She answered with another sigh so deep that it moved right through her and into him. He gathered her closer. "I'm glad." After a moment, he dared to ask. "What are you going to do next?"

She sighed. "I don't know."

"There is...help, especially for people with PTSD," he said gently, realizing at once it was the wrong thing to say.

She sat back, scooting to the far end of the sofa and wiping her eyes. "I'll fix things myself."

"You're plenty strong enough, Sage. I was just suggesting..."

"That I need to go see a shrink," she said, springing to her feet. "So he can analyze me or maybe give me some pills."

"No," he began.

She folded her arms across her chest. "But Captain Black doesn't need to do that."

The sarcasm bit at him. "I would talk to someone if I needed to."

"But you don't need to because you've got God on your side? In spite of what you've done to your brother?" Anger hummed in her voice. "I wonder why He's not on my side, then."

Trey searched for a way to put out the fire he'd inadvertently lit. "He is."

"If He was on my side He wouldn't have let Luis die. He wouldn't have let me have my arrogant way. He would have saved me from myself." The last phrase came out in a whisper.

"Sometimes He doesn't do that."

"He saved your brother."

Trey sighed. "Yes, but that wasn't because I deserved it."

She opened her mouth to answer but stopped, turned on her heel and walked away, taking the lantern with her and leaving him alone in the darkness.

FOURTEEN

When do I turn back into myself? Muscles taut as wire, Sage tried to stifle her sniffling as she slid between the cold sheets. She didn't understand why she'd twisted the sweet moment between them into something ugly. Trey was trying to help and she'd shoved him away on a tidal wave of anger that came out of nowhere. Strangest of all, she did not want him to go away, she realized. He was the one person she desperately wanted close, though she could not comprehend that desire either. Attraction? Yes. Something deeper? The thought scared her.

Careful not to wake Antonia by tossing on the squeaky bed, she clasped her hands together so hard her fingernails bit into the skin. Where to start? What to say? How could she possibly explain?

The thought filtered up through her heart, pushing by the darkness and cold that filled that space. "Come find me because I can't find You," she whispered, head spinning and tears flowing, hot, down onto the pillow.

She heard the rustle of blankets and found Antonia sitting up, dark eyes gleaming as she watched Sage.

"Sorry," Sage mumbled. "Did I wake you?"

Antonia might have shaken her head, but Sage couldn't tell in the darkness. "I thought I heard someone crying."

"Bad day," Sage managed.

"Barbara told me you were back from Afghanistan and it was…hard there."

Sage closed her eyes. "Yes. Hard."

"You're lucky to have someone who understands." Antonia paused and Sage realized she must be referring to Trey.

"He was the captain of the platoon where I was stationed."

"He's a man you can trust?"

Shame burned inside her for the anguish she knew she'd caused him only a short time ago. "Yes, he is," she said carefully. A man who should be trusted, and loved by someone who could treat him the way he deserved.

"Then hang on to him," she said, lying down on the bed again. "Most men are not worth loving."

"Like Derick?"

She hissed out a breath. "Like all men. The ones you can trust are rare."

"Antonia, how did you meet my cousin?"

Antonia rolled onto her back now, her tone softer.

"She was vacationing in Florida and I'd done some murals in a hotel there. She'd heard about my work and came to see it and hired me to consult on the Imperial."

"Long way to go from Florida to San Francisco."

"I needed the money. My sister…" Her voice trailed off. "I just needed the money."

"Rosalind said…" Sage hesitated.

She exhaled. "That I've been in trouble, and she's right. Barbara knew, but she let me keep my past mistakes where they belong…in the past. I won't ever forget that. It's part of the reason I was so determined to help her when I thought…well, you know what I thought."

Keeping the past in the past. Sage wished she was able to accomplish that feat. She felt a sudden overwhelming desire to see Barbara again, and her father and mother, her sister, Erika. If she could be with them, safely grounded again in the years of loving history between them, maybe that love would give her the power to put the past where it belonged. But she'd tried. How she'd tried to resurrect the person she'd been before, the Sage Harrington her family had known. She could not trust in her own strength.

Trey would say she had to trust in Jesus because He had already won the battle.

But how could she do that? How could she find the courage?

She recalled the way she felt, pressed into his chest, listening to the beating of his heart. So close. Steady. Reverberating down to the core of her, past the layers of darkness and fear.

"Yes," she whispered. "Trey is someone to hang on to."

And then the conversation was over. Movement from the other bed indicated Antonia had turned away, giving her back to Sage.

The ones you can trust are rare.

Trey Black was definitely one of the rare ones.

Somewhere between her encounter with Trey and the hours before dawn, she must have slept, awaking with a jolt and a pounding heart. She clutched the blanket, assessing, trying to remember how she'd wound up in a small hotel room, the cracked clock on the wall pegging the time at just before six. The curtains shrouding the window trembled slightly and she realized they'd had another aftershock.

Calm down, she told her hammering heart. Still, she knew the safest course of action was to get moving, just in case there was a need to evacuate. She sat up, rubbing the grit from her eyes, and walked to Antonia's bed.

"Another earthquake," she said softly. "We'd better get up, just in case."

There was no answer from Antonia, so she

reached a hand out to her shoulder, encountering only a soft mound of rumpled blankets.

"Antonia?" The sheets were cold to the touch. She padded out into the quiet hallway and into the lobby, where she found Trey heating water on the camp stove with Wally watching him from his perch on the arm of the sofa.

"Aftershock wake you?"

"Yes." Ignoring the flutter in her stomach when his eyes roamed her face, she got to the point. "Antonia isn't in her bed. I think she's left."

Trey didn't answer for a moment. "There's really nothing to keep her here, I guess. Awkward situation in view of the fact that she accused Derick of murder and Rosalind announced that Antonia was a liar. Maybe it's easiest on everyone if she did leave."

Sage paced the small room, arms folded against the chill. "I just feel like something isn't right."

Rosalind bustled in without shoes, hugging her soiled jacket around herself. "Derick is gone."

Sage stared. "When?"

"I just checked his room, the bathroom, the grounds. Nothing."

"They might have gone to get some air," Trey suggested.

"They?" Rosalind's mouth creased with worry lines as she heard about Antonia. "Oh, no. Maybe she had a knife, a weapon of some sort, and forced him to go with her."

"I think we would have heard him struggle, or cry out or something," Sage said, mind spinning.

"I'll go to the police," Rosalind said.

Trey took the pot off the burner. "Let's not get ahead of ourselves. Maybe they went back to the deli, or took a walk."

Rosalind nodded. "I'll get my shoes and see if I can find them."

"I'll go with you," Sage said.

"We'll go," Trey said, correcting her.

A flush of something like happiness and relief warmed her stomach. She hadn't driven him away completely and for that she was grateful.

Emiliano was just padding into the kitchen as they opened the front door. He stifled a yawn. "Are you leaving this early? It's not even sunup yet."

"Antonia and Derick have gone somewhere."

Emiliano raised an eyebrow. "That explains it."

Sage's gut clenched. "Did you see them leave?"

"I heard a noise a few hours ago. I thought it was more looters, so I grabbed my baseball bat and took a look around, but there was no one. Out the window I just caught sight of Mr. Long with a flashlight moving away from the hotel. Didn't see Antonia with him."

"That shoots down the theory that Antonia forced him to leave," Trey said.

Rosalind's eyes rolled. "I can't believe this. Like we haven't been through enough. Which way did he go?"

Emiliano pointed a finger in the direction of the ruined opera house.

Sage understood why Antonia had left, but she could not comprehend why Derick would have any reason to go back to the Imperial.

Antonia's earlier revelation came back to her.

I checked the shoes. They were covered in dirt and flecks of gold plaster. She swallowed the thick wave of fear. If the phone call from Barbara was fake…

Trey grabbed his pack and gave Emiliano the handheld radio that Derick had used earlier. "Contact us if either of them returns here."

Rosalind pulled on the shoes she'd fetched from her room. "Let's go before he does something stupid."

The moist air chilled Sage immediately. "What do you think he's up to, Rosalind?"

"Who knows?" she said over her shoulder.

"I think you do."

Rosalind flicked a quick glance at her and then away. "I have no idea." She quickened her pace over the slick cement, which was cracked and heaved up in places. Wally trailed behind her, leaping on dainty legs over chunks that blocked his way.

Trey moved close and put his arm around Sage's

shoulders. Her body reacted to the feel of his strength, the warmth that passed from his skin to hers. He whispered, "What do you think?"

She put her mouth to his ear, resisting a wild urge to kiss his neck. "I think she's covering for him. Derick's gone back in there for some reason and she knows what it is."

He stopped her then and she thought his breathing was a bit erratic much like her own.

"Sage, I don't want anyone back in that opera house. For any reason. It was a wonder that we all got out in one piece, and if Derick was crazy enough to go in there again, he's on his own."

"What if he was lying all along? If Antonia was right and Barbara is down there?"

His jaw muscles tightened. "Rubio told us Barbara called the station. She's fine. It's over."

She didn't answer but something deep down inside, the part of her that she used to rely on as instinct, told her that the situation was far from over.

Trey had an uncomfortable sense of déjà vu as they arrived outside the front entrance of the Imperial. It was just before sunup and the sky had edged from black to gray. There was no sign of Derick or Antonia and he did not intend to let Rosalind or Sage set one toe inside the wreck again. There were acceptable risks, and there was just plain stupidity. Though he could not explain Derick's odd behavior, if the guy wanted to go get himself entombed in his opera house, he could do it alone.

The doors were closed, a gap between them revealing how badly the building had shifted. Rosalind stepped under the yellow tape Rubio had tied across the doors and yanked on one. It opened with a hideous creak that set his teeth on edge.

She peered inside. "No sign that anyone has been here. Maybe they went back to the deli for some reason."

"Or decided to try to get back to the house on foot," Sage mused aloud.

"Why bother if the roads are going to reopen today?" Trey wished he hadn't added fuel to Sage's suspicions.

"Exactly." She looked over the top of Rosalind's head. "Are you sure there are no footprints in the dust?"

Trey didn't like her proximity. He was about to use his captain's voice when Wally pushed in between Sage's legs, barking madly. In a moment he was through the door, his barks now amplified.

"Wally," Trey called. "Come here."

The dog obeyed about as well as anyone else clustered on the sidewalk at that moment. He surged forward, oblivious to Trey's commands and now adding in a shrill whine to accompany the barking.

"Come here," Trey thundered. He caught sight of Wally's hind legs kicking up clouds of dust as he pawed at a new section of wall that had collapsed since the last time they'd clapped eyes on the lobby.

Trey elbowed past Sage and Rosalind. "I'll get him." Sage held a flashlight into the space as he headed for the dog.

"We're going to end up at the bottom of a pile of rubble, Wally." Trey tried to reach for Wally's collar, but all he got was a handful of hair off the trembling body. He moved in farther, brushing cobwebs off his face and trying not to inhale the filthy air.

Wally continued to work at a spot near the floor, which appeared to be nothing but a dark hole to Trey's eyes.

"Come on, dog. Let's get out of here." This time he got a grip on the animal, which whined pitifully and sent up a loud barking protest. As he slid Wally away, Sage's flashlight beam hit on something. A piece of rubber, he thought, until he bent closer.

No, not rubber.

He turned and handed the dog to Rosalind. "Hold him for a minute."

Her eyes rounded in fear. "Why? What did you find?"

He didn't answer, returning to the spot and confirming for himself that his eyes had not played tricks on him. Grasping the black rubberized sole, he gently pulled, hoping the motion would not bring the rest of the structure down on his head.

The thing in his hands was a pair of boots, attached to a soiled pair of legs. He continued to ease the legs free, an inch or two at a time, until he got one wrist clear of the mess. Kneeling, he checked for a pulse.

The cold skin told him before the terrible stillness. There was no pulse, no life, left in this victim.

Sage and Rosalind had taken a step, involuntarily perhaps, towards him.

"Who...?" Sage's lips were rounded into a horrified O. He grasped the boots once again and continued to pull the figure free until the face was visible, whitened with plaster.

Wally leapt out of Rosalind's hands and ran to the body of his owner.

"Fred Tipley," Sage breathed. "How come we didn't see him before?"

"He was in the storage room just behind the lobby wall. It probably collapsed because of the aftershocks."

Rosalind let out a low moan. "Horrible. How many has this earthquake killed?"

Trey bent closer, examining Fred's motionless face. "Not this one."

Sage jerked. "What do you mean?"

"He wasn't killed by a collapse." Trey pointed to a hole in the middle of a dark shadow on Fred's shirt. "He was shot. I think that's where the blood on Wally came from."

He did not allow himself to think about the little animal mourning next to his dying owner. All the smart scientist types said that dogs don't grieve. They were wrong.

"Oh, Fred," Sage whispered. "Who would want to kill you?"

The words hovered there as if held aloft by the shock that all three felt in that moment. Trey knelt next to Fred and did a cursory check. Minor bruises, a scrape on his hairy arm. Though his mind wanted to shy away from it, the truth shouted itself loud and strong in his ears. Fred had been murdered. Not by looters, he figured. What was there in the old wreck worth stealing?

Sage turned to Rosalind. "You said he left."

She shook her head, eyes round, mouth twisted. "He did. He must have gone back in for something. I feel sick."

Trey patted Fred's pockets and removed a crumpled five-dollar bill and a handful of change. There were no car keys. The other pocket yielded only a balled-up handkerchief and a half-inch-long oval pill. He rolled it around in his palm.

Sage shone the light on it and her face went so dead white, he grabbed her arm. "Deep breaths."

She sucked in some air and swallowed hard. "Trey, that's a prenatal vitamin. I remember them from my sister, Erika's, pregnancy."

He looked again at the pill, which he now saw

was bright pink in color. "Prenatal?" The word circled stupidly through his brain. An old man with a prenatal vitamin in his pocket.

Her eyes were no longer locked on the vitamin, but they were fixed on Trey's other hand, dirty from grasping Fred Tipley's shoes. He followed her horrified stare to the dirt that caked his fingers and the tiny flecks of gold that shone like sparks in the beam of light.

FIFTEEN

"Fred was in the basement before he was killed," Sage said, her stomach flipping over itself, cold shivers running through her.

"With prenatal vitamins in his pocket," Trey finished.

Sage imagined that time stilled at that moment, the air of the theater thickening around them, pressing the truth home. It could no longer be chalked up to her wild imagination or the product of her lingering trauma. "Barbara," she breathed. "Barbara is here. Fred was keeping her in the basement."

"But the phone call," Rosalind burst out. "How did that happen?"

"The cops are overwhelmed right now. They took a message that Barbara called, but it was probably someone using her cell phone. Maybe Fred had a woman friend make the call."

Rosalind passed a hand over her eyes. "This is a nightmare."

Trey grunted. "He hasn't been dead more than a few days."

"Barbara has been trapped down there the whole time." The realization sizzled through her. "Antonia was right. Derick wanted to get rid of her. Fred was working for him." It was what she'd known all along, but saying it aloud made her feel sick. Barbara's husband. The man she'd loved.

Rosalind's mouth thinned into a fierce line. "You're wrong. Derick wouldn't do that."

"Then why did he sneak out and come in this direction?"

"Someone else snuck out, too, remember? Antonia. He might have been following her," she snapped back. "Listen to me. I can't explain the details here, but I know Derick Long better than anyone alive. I am telling you he would not hurt his wife."

"He's an actor," Trey said. "He's paid to make people believe something that isn't true."

Rosalind's eyes flashed. "Don't patronize me, Captain Black. I'm a smart woman and I'm well aware that Derick is not the man you see on the screen. I'm telling you he didn't hurt his wife and that's because I know him inside and out."

Trey didn't back down. "Maybe you just think you do."

"I spent my share of time dazzled by the whole smooth talking, charmer persona, but you can't work for someone for fifteen years and not see the real person. You're wrong about him. You've just got to believe me."

"Not now," Sage said. Urgency burned inside her. "We can sort it all out later. For whatever reason, Fred had her trapped in the basement and the Imperial is flooding. We have to get her out."

Trey was already pulling on his pack. "Fastest way is to go back through the hotel tunnel and hope…"

Sage knew the rest. And hope it wasn't underwater along with Barbara. She forced herself to take several pictures of Fred's body with her phone for the police to use later. Was she preserving the image of the man who might have caused the death of Barbara and her babies? The thought made her skin prickle and she realized she was holding her breath.

Trey pulled a piece of fallen curtain from under a pile of rubble, sending dust motes roiling through the lobby. He draped it over Fred's body, gently pushing Wally away. Rosalind knelt and held out her hand to Wally, crooning, but the dog remained curled in a shivering ball at his fallen master's side.

"Emiliano," Trey called into the radio. "Get the police if you can." He told him about the murder.

Murder. Sage's mind was still foggy with disbelief. Derick was a killer. Why did it not seem real to her now, after she'd spent the past weeks worrying about that very scenario?

Trey shouldered his pack and called to Wally, who refused to come, so he scooped him up, murmuring soft words of comfort into his ears and kissing the top of his head. The image took her breath away, the muscle-bound soldier who she knew was hard as granite on the battlefield, cradling the little animal tenderly in his big hands. Part of her warmed inside, a place that had been cold and numb for what seemed an eternity. Trey was not perfect, he'd let down his brother and carried the shame of that with him just as she would always bear the burden for Luis. But he had moved on. Conquered that obstacle. Allowed himself to live and love again.

Her eyes swam, but there was no more time to consider the irony further as they emerged into the misty dawn. They retraced their steps back to the hotel where they met a grave-faced Emiliano.

"We need to get into the basement," Trey said. "What is the fastest way?"

"I only know one way and that's through the storage room at the end of the tunnel, the one you said was wedged closed."

"Then we'll have to unwedge it this time," Trey said.

Emiliano nodded and darted outside, returning

seconds later with a slightly rusty ax. "This will get you through the door, but if there's flooding…"

"I know. It may all be underwater." His eyes flicked to Sage.

She felt an unexpected sense of calm. "I understand what we're facing here."

He reached out a hand and she read the message in his face.

You don't have to come. I'll take care of it, and if she's alive I'll bring her back.

She let the pressure of his fingers squeeze strength and faith back into her. "I'm going to try to face it, however it turns out." She swallowed against a thickening in her throat, the fear licking at the edges of her certainty. She thought about Barbara and her babies, pictured Luis's fallen body, broken and dying. "I'm not sure I'm strong enough." She cleared her throat. "If I can't…can you go it alone?"

He surprised her with a smile that lit his whole face and quickened the pulse throbbing in her throat. "I'm pretty handy when things go bad, but I happen to know we're not alone in this anyway." He pressed the tips of her fingers to his lips, sparking trails of something like joy directly to her heart.

When she found her voice again, it was barely audible. "Because He's already overcome the world?"

Trey's smile broadened. "Without a doubt."

"I'm going to try to remember that."

With one final squeeze of her hand, he let go, snapping back again into Captain Black, the man who had made her heart flutter at their first encounter.

Rosalind clutched Sage's arm. "I'm going, too."

"Why?"

Rosalind blinked at the floor before answering. "I think Derick is down there."

"You know he's involved in Barbara's disappearance, don't you?"

Rosalind ran a hand through her hair, splaying the bangs into an untidy wave. "No, I know nothing of the kind," she said as she asked Emiliano for a pack and headed toward her room. "I'm just going to grab some things from my purse."

Emiliano soberly accepted a wriggling Wally from Trey. "He's been through a lot. Don't let him wander away, okay?"

"I'm only a temporary guardian, right?" Emiliano said, eyeing the dog with suspicion. "My wife has three crabby cats and they'd tear him apart, so I can't keep him."

Trey laughed. "No worries. Wally's got a home with me. He'll love the mountain cabin I'm going to build as soon as this disaster is over."

A lance of pain shot through Sage's heart. Trey would be gone soon. Of course. She hadn't been expecting anything else. The lightness in her soul evaporated.

So what's the problem, Sage? You didn't expect

him to stick around anyway. She checked her flashlight to make sure the batteries were working and ran to catch up with Trey's long strides as he headed down the hallway to the ladder.

Rosalind fell in behind, close as a shadow as they descended, the cold shock striking Sage's legs as she stepped off into water that was well over her knees. The sound of the waves lapping against the brick walls reverberated, echoing crazily and throwing off her sense of equilibrium. Her flashlight showed broken bits of wood floating by. Drops plinked down onto the surface, teasing ripples into the water, one finding a target on Sage's temple before sliding down her neck. They waded slowly, their feet stumbling on hidden obstacles as they progressed past the opening that had led them earlier to the elevator shaft.

Darkness, uncertainty, guilt and regret hummed inside her, as unexpected as the massive earthquake. She felt as if she was right back in Afghanistan, holding Luis's hand again as the life leaked out of him.

I'm sorry, so sorry.

Memories welled up to drown her. Ripples of fear working their way along her spine until she heard Trey's words rumbling through her memory.

...part of us stayed behind with the ones who didn't get to go home, a little bit will always be with

them because they blessed us and we won't forget that. I wouldn't want to.

She forced another image into her mind. This time it was Luis laughing, telling one of his famous cornball jokes that amused him no matter how many times he shared it. And she realized with a start that Trey was right, part of her would always be with Luis, just as his generous heart and gentle spirit would remain with her. Luis had blessed her. And it was a gift.

Tears stung her eyes as she felt the horror roll back from her heart. "Thank you, God, for Luis," she whispered.

Rosalind looked at her sharply. "What did you say?"

"Nothing," she said, turning away from Rosalind's probing light to wipe her eyes.

It was an extraordinary place to grab hold of that bit of peace, pressed in on all sides by danger and ruin, and as welcome as a light in the darkness.

Trey stopped at the storage room door and gave it an experimental kick. It was still firmly wedged, impervious to the rising tide of water. Sage held his pack and Rosalind shone the light on the door while he shouldered the ax.

"Step back," he ordered, earning a sniff of disapproval from both women. He cleared his throat and tried again. "Sorry. Step back…please," he corrected.

They sloshed back several paces, and he swung the ax at the door. As he swung again and again, he prayed to the rhythm of the strikes, asking for protection for Barbara and her babies and for Sage, if Barbara and her children had not survived the earthquake and ensuing flood. There was also the matter of a murderer on the loose, but he could not seem to rid his thoughts of the tenuous courage he'd seen in Sage back in the hotel. The hope it awakened in him eclipsed everything else and he desperately wished that what lay behind the door would not cause her to lose it.

The ax triumphed over the heavy wood and a hole began to appear, widening until the door disintegrated altogether. He put the ax aside and pushed through the water, which mercifully had not risen past his upper thighs. With all three of their lights combined, he could just make out the ceiling, a scant four feet above his head. The area smelled of rotten wood, probably from the shelving that both clung to the walls and floated in pieces in the water around him, and the tang of something familiar tugged at his senses. The basement itself spread out into two passageways, each marked by a once regal-looking stone arch, now ribboned with cracks and marred by missing stones. Beams of worm-eaten wood ran along the ceiling of both passages.

Slicks of iridescent color floated on the surface of the water.

Sage splashed by him, casting her light over the far wall. It sparkled with remnants of the gold paint long ago used to create an experience for theater-goers. "I don't see anything," she said.

"That's right," Rosalind agreed. "Absolutely nothing to indicate Barbara was held down here. It's all hogwash."

"Hogwash didn't kill Fred Tipley," Sage shot back.

Trey noted Rosalind didn't even try to respond to that one.

He examined the bits of debris bobbing around him for anything that would indicate Barbara had been there and came up with nothing. Sage splashed toward the two passageways. "We've got to go far-ther in." She cocked her head at Trey. "Which one?"

Rosalind pointed to the left tunnel. "That one."

Trey's senses prickled. "What makes you think so?"

"The right tunnel is boarded up about six feet back because of an earlier collapse."

Trey waded into the supposedly blocked tunnel. "No offense, but I'd like to see for myself."

Rosalind might have looked slightly uneasy, but Trey could not be sure in the dismal light. "Suit yourself," she said.

Keeping the flashlight out of the water, he edged into the tunnel. Above his head, he could see busy termites trailing along the old wooden beams and still the faint smell he could not put his finger on danced across his senses.

Sage splashed behind him and he risked a look. Her face was serious and anxious, but strong at the same time. Something swam by him and he jerked back.

Sage laughed. "Just a rat. He's not much bigger than Wally."

"Funny," he said. "Maybe I should take it home so Wally can have a pal."

They turned the bend in the tunnel and sure enough, a few feet back the tunnel was walled over with a heavy planked door. The bottom three feet was darkened by the water slapping against it.

"You see?" Rosalind said. "Just like I said."

Trey shone his light down to examine the iron knob. "I can go back and get the ax if we need to."

"Do—?" Sage stopped abruptly.

His muscles tensed. A shout? The three of them froze. All he could hear now was the sound of his own breathing, the irregular dripping of water. A clang came from somewhere he guessed was west of their location.

"It's coming from the other tunnel." There was no time for caution now. Trey fought through the water, causing waves that splashed up across his shirtfront. Sage tripped over something and went down, popping back up by the time he'd turned to help her. She stood, completely soaked.

"I'm fine. Keep going," she gasped, slicking her hair back from her face.

They made it to the main room and set off down the other tunnel. The water was still at thigh level as they churned along, passing stacked crates and rolls of canvas swollen and toppled, which Trey shoved out of their way. Along the top of the tunnel was a six-inch ledge of decrepit wooden shelving crammed with wooden boxes. He caught the glitter of feathers protruding from one broken box, and in another, a gleam of light-colored fabric that might have been an opulent costume in days gone by.

"Barbara wanted it all catalogued," Sage panted as they fought their way through the water.

"A colossal waste of effort if you ask me," Rosalind said, holding her pack. "It's all ruined by the years and damp, what the rats haven't gotten into."

Trey didn't respond, but he knew Rosalind was right. A bunch of decaying costumes couldn't be worth a nickel, and Barbara's passion to restore every inch of the place would be ruinously expensive. Rosalind and Barbara would be at odds over it. So would Derick and Barbara. And Antonia? He shoved a floating crate out of their way. He still wasn't sure how she fit into the whole mess. Keeping to the middle of the tunnel to avoid both the debris and the skittering rats that scurried along the wooden shelves over their heads, he zeroed in on a door at the end of the passage.

At first he thought it was closed, shut up tight like the other had been, but as they neared he saw it was held open about six inches by a section of metal rod. Above the rush of the water, he heard it again, a shout that sounded desperate or angry, he could not tell which. The moment he ducked under the rod and squeezed through the door, he nearly went down as a strong current almost took the legs from under him. He yelled a warning to Rosalind and Sage as he fought his way through the swiftly moving water.

In spite of the heads-up, Rosalind lost her footing and floundered. Sage and Trey grabbed hold of her, but it cost Sage the flashlight, which was whisked away by the flow before either of them could snatch it up.

Rosalind shook her soggy fringe of hair. "Thanks," she gasped. "What's going on in here?"

"There must be a lower level where the water is heading," Trey said, beaming his light. The chamber was similar to the other, complete with wooden shelves and a full complement of rats. The rear of the chamber was screened by a mound of interlocked debris, which had been a shelving unit at one time but now was a floating screen, collecting the detritus propelled along by the current. Something bumped against his thigh. It was metal, a gas canister.

A woman's voice sounded high and shrill from behind the debris. "Don't let go!"

The panic carried the words over the moving water and the pulse roaring in his own ears. Fighting the current as if it were the enemy itself, he churned through the dark mass, edging past the hulking ruins.

SIXTEEN

Sage tried to keep her body from being swept past Trey, who had stopped as if electrified. She looked around his broad shoulders and her heart leaped to her throat. Antonia was braced against a brick pillar as Derick tried to pull her away. Sage stumbled forward and Trey's light brought the tableau into clearer focus. Antonia was not trying to escape Derick Long, but to save him.

His lower body was immobile, trapped in something she could not see below the water. Only his upper torso rose above, his eyes so wide with terror that the whites showed eerily in the darkness.

"Help me," he shrieked. "Something is cutting into my legs."

Antonia clung to his wrists. "I can't hold on. He's slipping."

Sage and Rosalind splashed forward immediately, grabbing hold of his wrists just as Antonia lost her grip and fell back. Afraid to let go, Sage was relieved when Antonia erupted quickly from the water coughing and heaving in a breath.

"He fell through something," she gasped.

Trey threw his pack to Antonia and disappeared under the water. He emerged a moment later. "It's a floor drain. His leg is caught on some rebar. I'll have to cut him out."

He took a deep breath and disappeared back under the surface.

"Just hold on," Rosalind called.

Derick moaned. "I tried to fix it. I tried so hard."

Rosalind shushed him sharply. "There's nothing to fix. Quiet now."

Sage wanted to press, but as the minutes ticked by she grew more and more terrified that Trey had not returned. Sloshing closer, she tried to feel around for him, but her grasping fingers found nothing.

"He's not there," she said, seeing her own fear mirrored on Antonia's face.

Suddenly Trey burst upward out of the water, coughing and sucking in an enormous breath. "Water carried me past him down the spillway. I barely made it back." He wiped his face with the crook of his arm. "Stop moving," he barked at Derick.

"I can't, something is cutting into my legs, biting at me. It's the rats."

Rosalind looked at Sage. "I think he's delusional."

Trey moved to within a foot of Derick's face. "Listen to me, Derick. You stop thrashing around and I'll get you out. If you don't, you're going to drown here. Got me?"

The hard tone seemed to bring Derick back from the brink. He nodded meekly.

Trey tied a rope around an iron ring fixed into the wall and went under the water, and Sage could feel him fighting to keep from being swept through the floor drain again. Suddenly, Derick jerked under their grasp.

"One of my legs is free," he cried, breath coming in pants. Trey came up for air again.

"Hold tight, the water is going to work against us," he said.

Sage nodded and gripped Derick's wrist harder. Another movement from underneath and Derick's other leg came loose. Sage and Rosalind pulled Derick away from the drain, and Trey helped when he resurfaced again, but Sage noticed he paused, looking back toward the floor drain as he untied himself from the rope.

With painfully slow progress, they fought the tugging water until they reached the door and squeezed by. In the outer tunnel the water was slower, and all five of them stopped to catch their breath. Rosalind kept her arm under Derick's shoulders since he looked like he was about to collapse.

"Where's my cousin?" Sage said, panting. "Tell me what you did to her."

Derick leaned his head against the stone wall. "I will never ever set foot in this death trap again. I think it's haunted."

Sage moved close and stuck her face in his. "Tell me right now, Derick. Where is Barbara?"

He opened his eyes and stared at her as if they had never met. "Are we back to that again? She's in Santa Fe."

"Why did you come down here?" she cried, looking from Antonia to Derick.

Antonia's hands were shaking as she shoveled wet hair out of her eyes. "I heard him get up and leave the hotel. He was being so quiet and sneaky. I knew then that he really had done something to Barbara, so I followed."

Lifting his foot out of the water, Derick examined a set of deep scratches to his shin. "This theater. It's ruined my life," he moaned.

Rosalind took hold of his shirt with her free hand. "Enough, Derick. Don't be so melodramatic."

"We're still waiting on an explanation from Sly Steel here," Trey said, arms folded across his chest. "Why did you come back? And maybe you could explain about Fred's murder while you're at it?"

Derick's eyes opened wide. "Murder?"

"He was shot," Sage said, wondering if the reaction she saw was real. "Why did you come down here?"

"To cover it up," he half sobbed.

Rosalind shushed him again.

Sage felt her stomach drop to her feet. "To cover what up?" she said, a hitch in her voice.

She heard Trey's sudden intake of breath. "Oh, I see. I should have figured that out sooner."

"Figured out what?" she snapped.

"The gas cans." He shot a disgusted look at Derick. "I wondered why I kept smelling gasoline. You were going to burn down the Imperial. For the insurance settlement?"

Derick laughed. "The insurance payout wouldn't even come close to the money I've funneled into this dump. I just wanted to end it so Barbara wouldn't ruin us."

Sage's mouth dropped open. "You were going to torch the place? Why not just tell Barbara you couldn't afford it?"

"Because," Derick shouted, his voice rising with every syllable. "I love her and I didn't want to admit that I'm broke, okay? I made plans to burn the Imperial down, but the earthquake messed things up. I wanted to come back and remove the gas cans in case the insurance investigators or the police found them."

They all stared at him and Rosalind closed her eyes and sighed. "I told you," she said. "He loves Barbara. He'd never do anything to hurt her."

"You knew he was going to burn it?" Trey said.

Rosalind sighed. "I had my suspicions when I saw the muddy shoes."

"And that was okay with you?"

"Of course it wasn't," she spat, "but try talking him out of anything."

"But the prenatal vitamins," Sage pressed. "Fred was holding Barbara here."

Derick cocked his head. "What are you talking about? Fred Tipley? What did he have to do with Barbara?"

Rosalind looked away.

"Time for the truth," Sage said. "Rosalind, what was Fred Tipley's connection to Barbara?"

Derick pulled out of her grasp, steadying himself against the wall.

Rosalind straightened to her fullest height and gave them a look of scornful strength. "I'm sorry, Derick, but Barbara was having an affair and Fred Tipley was the one who helped her cover it up."

Trey had experienced shocked silence before, but this one was the capper. Even Sage appeared to be speechless. It was Derick who finally broke the spell.

"Barbara would never cheat on me, Rosalind," he sputtered. "You're completely wrong."

"I wish I was," she said miserably. "I overheard a phone conversation between Barbara and a man. It was obvious that they were…intimate."

"When was this?" Derick demanded.

"About a year ago."

"A year?" His eyes rolled in thought. Trey could see him doing the mental calculations. "About the time she became obsessed with restoring the Imperial," he finally said.

"Yes. She would meet him at the theater." Rosalind said. "Fred would arrange it and let him in. The business trips she took, the weekends without you. I'm sorry, Derick, but she was with another man."

Derick's mouth twitched. "Why didn't you tell me? You are my closest confidant, the person I can count on the most. Why didn't you tell me?"

"I didn't want to hurt you. I know your career slowdown has been hard to take, and I wasn't sure how much you could handle." She sighed, a pleading tone creeping into her words. "When she became pregnant, I thought things would change. She was going to be a mother and she was staying home more, skipping her weekends away. I thought she'd ended it with the guy."

"What's his name?" Derick whispered, hands balled into fists.

"I don't know."

"Yes, you do," he hissed. "Tell me right now."

"No, I didn't want to know. When she went to

Santa Fe, I was hoping she would get her head together and come home and commit to your marriage. I don't know anything about having kids." Her face grew sad. "But I'd always heard that it changed a person, being a mother."

"Maybe she was going on the trip to meet him," Derick said, voice thick with rage. "Maybe she found someone else to bankroll her theater project. Someone with a deeper wallet than mine."

"I'm sure that wasn't what happened," Rosalind said, but her voice betrayed uncertainty.

Trey tried to put the pieces into place. "Why the prenatal vitamin in Fred's pocket?"

Rosalind shrugged. "Leftover from an earlier time? I can't say for sure. I wanted to fire him, but Barbara wouldn't hear of it. The only thing I could do was forbid him to allow anyone into the theater, but Barbara's orders always countermanded mine."

Derick collapsed then, sliding down the wall until he hit the floor, shoulder-deep in the water.

Rosalind cried out and grabbed at him.

Trey hoisted him up in a fireman's carry. He was completely limp, blood dripping in rivulets from his injured leg. "He's in shock. We need to get him out after I bandage this."

With the women's help, he got Derick propped awkwardly on top of a crate. Rosalind supported his back while Trey fished a roll of plastic-wrapped gauze from his pack.

"Hold the light?" he asked and Sage waded forward and trained the flashlight on Derick's wound. He knew her mind was not on the first aid but struggling through the revelation from the past few minutes.

Barbara's affair.

Derick's attempted arson.

Antonia's stubborn belief that the actor was a killer.

Rosalind's equally determined opinion that he wasn't.

And Fred, killed by a looter? Some unidentified squatter? The man Barbara was having an affair with?

He started at the ankle, just above Derick's sock, wrapping loops of gauze around the wounds, replaying the past few minutes in his mind.

I think it's haunted.

He got to his feet wondering if he should trust his senses or his logic.

He might still be in the grip of paranoia born in battle.

Sage stared at him. "What is it?"

He turned to Derick and shook his shoulder. "Derick, can you hear me?"

Rosalind pushed Trey's hand away. "Stop it. He's hurt. We have to get him out."

"I need to ask him something." Trey crouched down to look into Derick's half-open eyes. "You said you thought the theater was haunted. Why did you say that?"

His head rolled back and forth. "When I was stuck in the drain I heard noises, moaning and wailing. I hate this place. I hate it." He slumped against Rosalind, who tried to chafe some warmth back into his arms.

"He's nuts," Antonia said.

"I wouldn't argue under normal circumstances." Trey applied some smelling salts from his pack, which revived Derick enough that he was able to stand with Rosalind's support.

Trey made his decision abruptly. "Can you three get him out? Retrace your steps back to the ladder." He handed Antonia the radio. "You should be able to contact Emiliano as you get closer. Call him if you run into a problem."

Sage grabbed his arm. "Wait a minute. Where are you going?"

"I need to check something."

Sage blocked his way. "Don't shut me out of it. We've been through enough by now, haven't we?"

He kept his voice low and even. "Just want to take a look down there."

Rosalind began to splash across the floor with Derick. "I could use some help here. He's heavy."

Antonia reluctantly positioned herself underneath his other arm.

"Not you," Rosalind snapped. "I need a man's muscles."

"Well, you're stuck with a woman's, so deal with it," Antonia snarled.

"I'm staying with you," Sage said to Trey.

"Rosalind and Antonia need you."

"They can handle it." She moved closer so he could see the curve of her lips, the soft, silky skin of her cheeks. "I'm not going to throw a fit and demand you fill me in this time. I'm just asking. Please tell me, Trey."

Antonia, Rosalind and their injured patient were several yards away now. He weighed the decision. Tell her and risk stirring up a swirl of emotions that would probably lead to nothing? Or keep it to himself and get her out of the Imperial as soon as possible? The uncertainty created arcs of tension in his gut. In the army he was always sure of himself, confident in his ability to lead. A planner, a commander, a winner.

Years before, when he'd let himself get sucked into gang life, he'd come home late one night and found Dallas still awake, sneaking cookies from the cabinet and eating them by the light of a stubby candle. With the scent of alcohol still on his breath, he'd looked at Dallas, the little kid with trust shining in his eyes. Dallas was an innocent, removed from the dark world of petty crime, violence and drinking. Trey should have gotten out before that life could get its hooks into his younger brother.

It seemed in that moment in the darkened kitchen, he'd had a choice. He made it and he'd abdicated his role as leader. He'd been trying to make up for it every day since. Now, as he looked into her eyes, he saw that she, too, trusted him, not the army captain, but him, Trey Black, the man with a full complement of sins and foibles, the man who had failed his brother. It warmed him inside and he swallowed back the unaccustomed tide of feeling. The question was, how much would he reciprocate?

She'd been through so much and he did not know if one more disappointment would be the proverbial straw that broke her. All he knew in that moment was that he did not want her to walk away, to go through whatever lay ahead on her own. "Sage…"

He spoke softly, pulling her close and trying to keep his senses from being addled by the softness of her body against his. "When I got sucked down through the drain, I thought I heard something or someone."

Her lips parted and she inched closer until his skin prickled. "What do you mean?"

"I thought I imagined it, but Derick heard it, too."

She stiffened in his arms. "Are you saying what I think you are?"

He whispered in her ear, "Someone is down there in the drainage system."

SEVENTEEN

Sage's legs refused to cooperate for what seemed like minutes. Shivers coursed up and down her spine, though she tried her best to hide it from Trey. They sloshed to the door, a gas can floating by, bobbing lazily. Barbara was all she could think about. It was too far-fetched to believe her cousin was trapped in the drainage pipes, but if Trey was right and someone was down there…

"Could it be your brother? You said he was going to check out the storm drains again."

"Don't know, but I need to find out."

Rosalind's voice carried over the sound of Sage's beating heart. "You two aren't really going down there, are you?" she shouted.

"Go on," she called back. "Get Derick to a doctor. We'll follow as soon as we can."

"You're both crazy, you know that?" came the peevish response.

Rosalind was probably right. Sage tried to move as fast as her chilled limbs would allow.

Trey pushed through the door once again and they slogged their way to the place where Derick had been stuck.

Trey took a breath and sank under the water, leaving Sage to listen to the sounds of rats clicking overhead and the soft clank of the flotsam bumping together in the dark void. Thirty seconds later he came up, heaving in a breath.

"The opening is circular, about two feet wide. Through it there's a chute that leads down to a spillway and flattens out from there, which is as far as I went earlier, but I couldn't see any farther."

Sage nodded. "We swim through the opening and down the chute."

"That's about the only way," he said. "Water's moving at a pretty fast clip. Scared?"

Her instinct was to lie, but her mouth took a different tact. "Terrified."

He started to respond, but she cut him off. "Scared or not, there is no way I'm leaving Barbara, your brother or whoever that poor soul is to drown in the darkness. I'm going to do this."

Something like respect shone in his eyes, or so she imagined, the kind with which he had regarded his fellow soldiers, the pride she hadn't realized she'd craved until just that moment.

He stood tall, defying the chaos that swirled around them. "You would have made a fine soldier, ma'am."

She laughed. "If the captain would only do things my way and quit insisting on giving me pesky orders."

He chuckled and she found herself moving to him, swept close. Tentatively she put her hands on his shoulders, running them up to his cheeks, wiping away the water from his temples, forehead, the strong planes of his cheek, the smooth curve of his lips. He closed his eyes and, standing on tiptoes, she pressed her mouth to his.

His military posture melted into an embrace and he returned the kiss with such intensity it took her breath away. Delicious currents of warmth cascaded through her until Trey pulled back, his expression full of half wonder and a good measure of panic. "Was that for luck?" he said, voice hoarse.

Suddenly she didn't know. Her mind was playing tricks on her, her fear pushing her into the arms of a man who was only there by happenstance, only doing his duty, a man whom she had openly defied. Uncertainty pooled in her stomach and spilled upward into her lungs. "Sure, just for luck," she said, stepping back into the shadows. "You first?"

He paused a minute, as if he wanted to say something. Instead he pulled off his pack. "I'll check the rope."

She tried to steady her breathing while he set to work, refastening the rope around his waist. Why had she kissed him? Why had he let her? She felt slightly sick at her own boldness and what he must now think of her.

"Wait for me to yell," Trey said. After another searching look, which she avoided, he ducked under the water and shimmied through the hole, carrying his pack in front of his body to keep it from being caught.

She waited, listening over the rippling water, trying to pull her mind away from the tingles left over after her ill-advised kiss. On the shelves above, she saw several gas canisters that Derick had not had time to remove.

She did not fault him for not having the courage to disappoint Barbara. She'd learned that her own supply of bravery had dried up promptly after Luis died in her arms. Understanding his failure made her feel the tiniest bit better about her own. She could almost relate to Rosalind, who couldn't bear to break Derick's heart with word of his wife's infidelity. If it was true that Barbara cheated on him… if any of it was true. The facts were blurring together in her mind the longer she stood there, cold and covered with goose bumps. Had it been a full minute yet?

She felt something bump against her leg and she bit down a cry. From overhead came a sharp crackle, maybe from a living thing, maybe just the wood settling around her. Fear caught flame inside and began to gnaw away at her confidence.

She forced herself back in time.

You would have made a fine soldier, ma'am.

She recalled the warmth of his arms holding her with tenderness that might be nothing more than her own imaginings. She busied herself breathing in and out, wishing she had not lost her flashlight.

Time dragged on. She began to think about the possibility that Trey had gotten into trouble, perhaps snagged on a protruding rod, knocked unconscious and sucked under the water.

Another minute gone. She shuffled next to the drain and shoved her hands into the water, feeling for the rope which was still stretched taut. She tugged on it, praying for a return pull. Nothing.

The what-ifs shook through her like the aftershocks that rocked the city. Sucking in a breath, she dropped to her stomach into the water and peered into the hole. She could see that the drain ended abruptly, plunging away into darkness. Trey was down there somewhere. Caught or knocked unconscious. She should get help. Resurfacing, she sucked in the musty basement air and took two steps toward the door until a surge of determination, stronger than the current, overrode her common sense.

This time she would not watch another man she cared about die.

This time, she would put another's life above her own.

Please, God, she managed as she once again sank into the water, and before she had time to re-think the idea, she held her breath and pushed her-self through the hole.

Trey tried to right himself. The drain hole shot him down a tube into a torrent of water that kept him rolling and tumbling until the rope snapped tight, jerking him back, imprisoning him at the bot-tom of the spillway as the water thundered around him.

He fought against his nature not to suck in a breath as he scrambled to find a foothold on the slippery cement. Finally, his boots hit solid sur-face and he struggled to his feet, keeping his head tucked to avoid the low ceiling. The water was lower, only shin-high, flowing past him on its way out into the darkness. He wanted to see if his flash-light worked and check out the surrounding area, but his thoughts were fixed on Sage.

"Sage!" he hollered. His words were buried under the sound of the roiling water, but he shouted again, louder.

He didn't think even the drill sergeant he'd had at boot camp, whom they'd referred to privately as D.S. Foghorn, could make himself heard over that cacophony. The only option would be to climb back up the tube until he got closer to the drain and shout again for all he was worth. He began to fight his way hand over hand, feet slipping on the slime-covered cement as he hauled himself upward. One meter of progress and he was panting, muscles burning from fighting the water that threatened to tear him off the rope.

He kept his mind on Sage. On that kiss, the one he still felt from his toes to his mouth and everything in between. Should he focus on that sign of tenderness that thrilled him to the core or the fact that she'd pulled away, regret showing plainly in her face?

Strange times, Trey. People in foxholes did uncharacteristic things that they would never contemplate during peacetime.

The stress of the situation brought on the need to be close, that was all. It was clear in the way she'd looked distressed after, as if she wished she could erase the moment altogether.

Water beat at his face and chest as he fought his way along.

Halfway up the tube, he paused to yell again into the darkness. He wondered if he should be telling her to forget it, to head back with the others. He had not heard anything that indicated Barbara's presence. He opened his mouth to holler just as a dark shape came hurtling out of the tube, crashing into him and knocking him over. He spiraled backward into the rush of water, scraping his elbows and knees.

He grabbed at the mass that passed him, fingers grasping sodden material, holding on with all the strength he possessed.

Sage's arms flailed as she fought off the pounding water. He'd gotten hold of the back of her sweatshirt.

"Grab on to me," he shouted.

She turned toward him, wide-eyed, thrashing.

He struggled to maintain his grip on her, praying the rope would hold as they were dragged down the spillway. It was like a twisted version of the water rides the kids enjoyed back home as they skidded over the concrete channel.

She thrashed some more before she got her body oriented in the right direction and her arms went around him, holding tight.

With a rib-creaking jerk the rope snapped taut at the bottom of the spillway, and this time it was nearly impossible to right himself with Sage's weight fastened to his middle and his pack sandwiched between them. Somehow he managed to once again find his footing and stand, knee-deep in the cascade, helping Sage to do the same. He half-pulled, half-dragged her away to the calmer water at the periphery, pressed against the damp stone walls. He freed his flashlight from his back pocket and shone it on her.

She was trembling, looking impossibly small, breathing fast. "I'm okay," she panted.

"Got tired of waiting?"

"I figured you'd had plenty of time."

He grinned. "I guess I did." He hugged her, allowing himself to press her body to his just for the briefest of moments, to assure himself she was there, safe and sound. When he reluctantly let her go, she wiped her hands over her face, clearing the droplets that collected on her hair and eyelashes.

"Where are we?"

He beamed the light around, shining it on the ceiling that was a scant five feet high. They were in some sort of water runoff system. Underneath their feet was cement, but his light revealed that farther ahead the surface sloped downward, morphing into a stone tunnel.

Sage chewed her lip. "This is too much."

"What is?"

She shook her head, showering him with drops of water. "Barbara's goal was to see every major opera house in the world. Her favorite is the Paris Opera House. You know, the one with the underground lake? Where the phantom hid out?"

"What phantom?"

"You never saw *The Phantom of the Opera?*"

"I'm more of a country and western kinda guy. Opera isn't my thing."

She laughed and splashed away toward the stone tunnel. "Well, if my cousin was trapped down here, she would spend the time exploring and trying to find a way out, not twiddling her thumbs."

"Exploring?" Trey secured his pack over his shoulders. "Women who are extremely pregnant go exploring?"

Sage called back over her shoulder, "Only one way to find out."

Trey caught up and splashed along behind Sage, ducking low enough for his taller frame to fit. The walls were cracked and trails of moss clung in the fractures. The extent of the old Imperial surprised him. "Derick would have to take a loan the size of the national debt to renovate this place."

She shot him a look. "True, but burning it down was not the answer."

Certainly cheaper than trying to fix it. He decided to keep that thought to himself. He still could not wrap his mind around the idea that the old relic was priceless. It was a theater where people pretended to be someone else and put on shows. It was not a cathedral or, say, an FT-17 tank, like the Five of Hearts, a full-track, steel-bodied monster that had overrun the German lines after taking over a thousand hits. Now that, he thought, ducking under a fractured beam, was an artifact worth every penny paid for restoration.

He was still contemplating the Five of Hearts when the smell of mildew made his nostrils burn and the tunnel ended abruptly. They stepped through into a chamber that did indeed feature an underground lake, though it was merely a collection point for water runoff no more than five meters across. He imagined there must be a drain at the bottom somewhere, which had been blocked due to the earthquake and caused the water to pool. Hard to say how deep, but he estimated no more than three meters, tops. All around them rose walls faced with stone, intersected by a series of catwalks that clung to the sides, some collapsed, their wooden poles hanging brokenly down toward the black water.

A desperate moan echoed through the chamber. Sage clutched Trey's arm. Slowly he circled the light around the cavern, over the still water, along the stone walls and across the broken catwalks. Something shone in the beam.

Trey did not believe in phantoms, but something moved on the catwalk to their left, something white and eerie.

Something human.

EIGHTEEN

Sage couldn't speak as the thing emerged on the catwalk above them. Her skin prickled when the tortured moan came again, and for a moment she had the impulse to run as fast and as far as she could.

A hand poked through the wooden railings of the catwalk, the fingers long and thin, curved into claws.

Trey raced up the rickety stairway before she could react.

"Someone's hurt," he called as he charged up the ladder. Sage finally fought through the shock and sprinted after him. The moans were cries of pain, which she would have figured out earlier if they weren't in such a bizarre location.

She emerged through the square opening onto a narrow wood-planked landing not more than three feet across. A crumpled bundle lay a few paces away, whimpering now.

Sage squeezed past Trey, who had knelt down

next to the figure, wedging his flashlight between the railings.

Wild black hair, a mouth twisted in agony, white full skirt and what had been a neat jacket ruined and soiled. Her cousin Barbara clutched the railing with one hand and her distended stomach with the other.

Sage dropped to her knees, overwhelmed. "Barbara. I've been looking for you." Tears stung her eyes as she realized her worst fears had been true. Barbara had indeed been imprisoned in the bowels of her beloved opera house, alone and terrified. "Who did this to you?"

Barbara started to answer, but her words morphed into a shriek of pain.

"She's in labor."

Sage looked dumbly at Trey. "Labor?"

His face was dead serious. "Yes. She's having the babies. Now."

Sage stopped herself from repeating the word *now.* Instead she swallowed hard and tried to force her brain to digest the facts. Her cousin's agonized cries seemed to derail any logical thought she might have had. Finally she forced her mouth into action. "Do you know how to deliver babies?" she croaked.

"We're going to find out," he said.

The dark walls blurred in front of Sage's eyes. They could not possibly be responsible for three lives here in the filthy underground chamber. Barbara's babies could not be born without the benefit of doctors and sterile sheets. She pulled out her phone and checked it. No signal. No help from above. How could they bring tiny fragile infants into the world now?

Trey was rummaging in his pack. He found a spray antiseptic and doused his hands and hers.

"We're not really going to do this, are we?" she whispered.

"No choice," he grunted. "It isn't going to wait."

Her mouth went bone-dry. "What—what should I do?"

"For the moment, hold her hand and pray."

Pray. It seemed the only thing that made sense. Sage knelt next to Barbara and took her hand, clutching the cold fingers in her own. "It's going to be okay, Barbara. We're going to help you." She began to speak prayers for her anguished cousin, for safety for the emerging little lives, for a supply of courage that she did not seem to feel. The prayers flowed naturally, as if she'd been on close terms with God all the time.

"The babies," Barbara moaned, squeezing Sage's hand in a death grip.

Trey looked up from his examination. "Got one crowning. Time to push, Barbara." He pulled off his bootlaces and laid them beside him, along with a pair of first-aid scissors.

Barbara only groaned again until Sage knelt

close. "Push now. You've got to push your babies out. Come on." She positioned Barbara's head on her knees and elevated her shoulders a little. "One, two, three."

Barbara grimaced as she managed to bear down and her entire body stiffened with pain. Just when Sage thought she could not possibly continue, Barbara went slack and Trey caught the baby girl in his hands. He quickly wiped her off with a corner of his shirt, tied the cord with the bootlace, snipped it and handed her to Sage. "Here. Find something to wrap her in."

Startled, she snatched the bundle and peered down into the tiny eyes that blinked back at her from a little wrinkled face before the baby started to cry. The sound was thin and small in the cavernous space, but it was sweet as a song, a melody of life in a lifeless place. Sage automatically began to jiggle the infant up and down like she had done with her sister's baby while she stripped off her sweatshirt, wishing it was dry. None of her clothes were dry and neither were Trey's. Barbara's garments were ragged, so the sweatshirt was the only option. She held the baby close, hoping her own body heat would keep it warm.

Barbara's hands balled into fists and a cry escaped her lips as the second baby began to crown. Sage cradled the girl in one arm like a football, while she found Barbara's hand with the other, waiting for Trey to give the signal to push again.

"Deep, slow breaths, Barbara."

She watched Trey's handsome face crease into consternation. Something fluttered deep inside her stomach as Trey caught her eye.

"Cord wrapped around the neck," he said, voice low. "I can't get my fingers under it. They're too big. Can you try?"

Sage's body went numb. *No, I can't. I'm too terrified to do anything.* But she knew doing nothing could mean the baby would die and possibly Barbara as well. Forcing herself to nod, she eased out from underneath Barbara and handed the bundled baby to Trey, who held on to her as if she was made of delicate spun glass. He used one arm to support Barbara's head.

Sage knelt between Barbara's knees and squirted more disinfectant on her hands before she tried to free the baby's neck from the strangling umbilical cord. She'd thought the cord would be fragile, a tissue-like thread that connected mother and child. Instead she discovered a tough, rope-like length cinched around the baby's neck. Panic surged up her spine when the cord remained tight in spite of her efforts, the baby's coloring turned strangely dusky in the weak light. *God, please, please, please.* Again and again she tried to tug it away.

Try as she might, she could not get the cord free from around the baby's neck. Now her hands were trembling violently. "I can't get it off, but I'll try to loosen it."

"Whatever you have to do to keep the airway open," Trey said. His voice was quiet, reassuring.

Trying to control her own shaking, she inched her first finger under the cord and eased it inch by inch until it hung more loosely around the baby's neck. "Okay, Barbara." *Okay, God.* "Let's have the baby." *Please save this child.* Panic prickling her skin, she held her breath and waited to see if God would save this tiny life or take Barbara's second baby home before it had the chance to experience even one small breath.

Trey's heart thundered in his chest as he squeezed Barbara's shoulders with one hand and juggled her daughter in the other. His whole being was riveted on Sage and the tiniest nuances of her expression—fear, concentration, hopefulness—as she tried to keep the cord from strangling the baby as it came through the birth canal. Prayers crashed through his mind like waves.

Time stood still, marked only by the faraway dripping and Barbara's ragged breaths. Then suddenly Sage surged forward, catching the newly birthed boy and holding him up into the circle of light. Her mouth went slack.

"He's not breathing," she whispered.

Trey's mind reeled to think of what advice to give, but Sage moved without him, turning the baby over, cradling his head in her palm and rubbing his back vigorously.

He saw from her face it had not worked. She propped the limp infant on her thighs, wiping his mouth and nose with her sleeve and tapping the bottom of his feet. "Please breathe, little baby," she cried.

The tension in her body told him before her stricken look. The infant was still not breathing.

"The baby," Barbara whispered. "My baby."

Trey lowered her and placed the little girl in her arms before he moved to Sage, who was staring into the face of the perfect boy. He had never tried CPR on an infant and the thought of his big hands on those delicate ribs made his gut tighten. He might make matters worse if that was even possible. No choice, he had to act.

He reached to take the baby from Sage when her hand shot out, stopping him.

"Wait." She put her cheek down close. "I think he's breathing." She tilted the baby's head back a small fraction and the baby sucked in a gurgling breath, coughed and let out a robust wail.

The joy in Sage's eyes and her wondrous smile lit his soul. He found himself grinning hugely, awash in awe. This life, this moment, in this foul place,

God had met them where they were and given them a miracle. Best of all, Trey knew from the happiness shining on Sage's face that she knew it, too.

"He's okay, Barbara. Your son is okay," he told her.

Barbara's sigh of relief mingled with their own.

Sage reached out one hand to him and he took it. Palm to palm, fingers intertwined, they allowed themselves a brief moment to mark the divine gift they had received, two lives birthed from the belly of a ruined opera house. He had no doubt it was the finest performance the old theater had ever produced.

He took a soggy flannel shirt from his pack and squeezed the water out as best he could before he handed it to Sage and she wrapped the baby, putting him gently on Barbara's chest to join his sister.

Barbara's eyes were closed, but she held the babies tight under her chin, tears flowing down onto their damp heads.

Sage made sure Barbara was as comfortable as possible and Trey checked her pulse, which was steady and strong.

He moved aside so Sage could kneel next to Barbara. She began to talk quietly to her cousin, telling her how beautiful the babies were, counting all their fingers and toes and reporting every detail to Barbara, who was too exhausted to answer.

Trey looked over the glimmering expanse of

water and tried to piece together an exit plan. Barbara was not strong enough to go anywhere, and he could not risk taking the infants up the rope, the way they had come. He squinted into the darkness, feeling the brush of cool air from the rear of the cavern. It must lead to the same system of tunnels that Dallas used to enter the theater, hence there must be a way out, but he could not risk the lives of four people on a what-if.

He felt Sage's hand on his lower back and as he turned, she fell into his embrace as if it were natural, as if they had not had a lifetime and a war between them. He kissed the top of her head.

"You did great," he said.

"You did, too, but it wasn't us."

He smiled into the darkness and gathered her close. "No, it wasn't." He wanted to stay like that, to keep her pressed close forever, but he felt the time ticking away, so he pulled her to arm's length.

"I need to go back. Get help."

She chewed her lip. "I will stay here with Barbara."

"I think you found that brave woman inside you," he said, tipping her chin up and wishing there was enough light for him to see the incomparable beauty of those blue eyes.

"Thanks for helping me with that," she said.

"Anytime." He went over the route. "I don't know

how quickly I can get back here. I'll leave the pack with you. There's water and…"

"Candy," she said with a laugh.

"That, too." He did not give voice to his biggest concern, that Barbara might begin to hemorrhage or experience some other complication. "Keep her sipping water if you can, and stay put."

She nodded. "I won't even bother with 'be careful.'"

He shrugged. "I'm always careful." He should have walked right down the catwalk ladder then, instead he pulled her close one more time and whispered in her ear, "Be here when I get back. Promise."

She leaned back to look in his eyes, a confused, half-panicked expression on her face, and he knew he'd blown it. He let go. *Strange times, that's all. She doesn't share your feelings.* And frankly, he didn't blame her. Three days ago he'd struggled between anger, outrage and attraction toward Sage Harrington. Now he could hardly bear to let her out of his sight. Emotional whiplash.

He cleared his throat. "I'll be back as soon as I can."

She nodded solemnly and knelt again next to Barbara while he hurried down the ladder. Just before he ducked into the stone tunnel, he looked up again and saw them both silhouetted in the weak glow of the flashlight. He thought he might have heard the gurgling cry of one of the babies, or maybe both.

How could he stand the responsibility, when he had made such a mess of it with his own flesh-and-blood brother? His breath seemed to crystallize in his lungs. Four lives, completely dependent on him. The weight of it nearly choked him.

He's already overcome the world, remember, Trey? All you have to do is overcome this labyrinth of cement and steel. Physical obstacles were something he could deal with. *Move it, Black.*

He jogged up the slope and into the stone tunnel, keeping his head low and avoiding uneven patches as best he could. The air grew warmer as he rose. Back in the lower level he knew the women and both babies would be cold and that spurred him to go even faster. He made it back across the spillway to the rope, splashing through the water without pause.

Seizing the rope, he looped it around his arm and tensed for the ascent until an odor assailed his nostrils. He stopped, peering upward toward the top of the rope. Mingled there along with the sprays of water was a wisp of smoke.

Acrid smoke that smelled of gasoline and burning wood.

NINETEEN

Sage still felt the surreal wash of feeling at all that the last few hours had stirred up. Barbara was alive and cradling two perfect babies. Below them, the lake rippled and gurgled as if it was composing a soothing lullaby for the infants born under such difficult circumstances. The divine nature of the miracle still sparked through her consciousness and she knew Trey had felt it, too.

Be here when I get back. Promise.

Had he meant something besides a stern warning for someone with a history of not following orders? She thought so, imagined she'd heard the throb of emotion in his words, but her senses were so muddled, she could not trust them.

"Sage?" Barbara whispered. "How are we going to get the babies out?"

Sage was encouraged that Barbara felt strong enough to talk. "We're going to stay right here until Trey brings back help." She waited a beat to see if Barbara's eyes would remain open. They did and

Barbara handed her the little girl. "I'm going to name her Sage."

Sage's eyes filled with tears. "That is the nicest thing I've ever heard."

Barbara's eyes clouded. "He put me in here. Chloroformed me and when I woke, I was locked up." Tears spilled down her face. "Caged like an animal. He shoved food in through a door in the back, and then locked it again."

"Who, Barbara?"

"Fred Tipley."

"Why would he do that?"

"I thought he was going to ask Derick for ransom, for the safe return of his wife and babies, but day after day passed and he didn't release me. Then there was that terrible earthquake and I thought…" She swallowed. "I thought no one would even know I was here. How did you figure out I was in the Imperial?"

"I didn't for a long time." She weighed her words carefully. "Derick told me you were in Santa Fe, but I thought it was so strange that you'd travel so close to the delivery date, so I was poking around when the earthquake hit."

"Santa Fe?" She gaped. "Why would he say that?"

Sage took a breath. "I don't know. I thought…I thought he'd done something to you."

Barbara's mouth fell open. "No, no. Derick loves me and the babies. He would never hurt us."

Sage didn't voice her inner thoughts. *He was going to burn down your opera house.* "We'll straighten it all out later." She kissed the feathery brows of the baby in her arms. "Why don't you make Sage her middle name? You can name her Elizabeth after your mother. Elizabeth Sage sounds perfect."

The distraction did not quite erase the worried crease on Barbara's forehead. "I heard someone in the drain. Who was that?"

"Derick."

Her face lightened. "You see? He came back to find me. He would never hurt me."

Sage busied herself pulling the sweatshirt closer around the baby and handing Barbara the bottle of water. "Take a sip."

Barbara shook her head. "I don't want any."

Sage spoke sternly. "You have to stay strong for these babies, so drink up."

Barbara took a small swallow, but Sage knew she was readying another question about Derick, so she stepped away, jiggling the baby up and down as she surveyed the lake beneath them. A shadow danced along above them on the ceiling, which, she supposed, was actually the lowest floor of the opera house.

A bat, she thought at first. An insect of some kind?

No, she thought, swaying her arms to comfort the child. It was a swirling shadow of smoke. Her stomach clenched. Smoke. All the wooden shelves, the broken beams and tattered canvases.

The Imperial Opera House, like those magnificent buildings in 1906, was on fire.

Panic rooted her to the spot. For several moments she did not realize that Barbara was talking to her.

"What is it? What?"

She could not lie to her cousin. "Smoke. I think there's a fire in the Imperial, somewhere on the upper floors."

Barbara let out an anguished cry and struggled to sit up. "We have to get the babies out."

Sage knelt next to her. "Trey will be back with help in time."

"You don't know that."

It was true. She didn't. Her fear was a cold, heavy mass inside her. "You said there was a door, where was it?"

She blinked. "I was drugged, I don't remember clearly."

Sage handed the baby to Barbara. "I'll be right back." Her feet practically flew down the ladder. At the bottom she skirted the lake, picking a trail around rubble and soggy patches of foul-smelling ground. In the rear, concealed behind a massive cement block, she found what she was looking for, a square opening that led away into the darkness.

It had been blocked at one time by a door, which now hung crookedly, easy to push aside on broken hinges. Finally, a helpful side effect from the earthquake.

But was it an escape? Or a dead end that would leave them farther away from the help that Trey was bringing?

She realized her hands were balled into fists, nails digging into the palms. Had Trey gotten trapped in the fire? The thought made her head spin.

Be here when I get back. Promise.

If he did make it back and found them gone...

Indecision cut at her insides, growing along with the volume of smoke that now undulated in eddies under the ceiling. She could not wait. They would die of smoke inhalation.

Praying her decision was the right one, she hurried back to Barbara.

"I think I found a way out. We've got to go."

Barbara nodded, already offering the babies to Sage before she tried to stand. Face lined with pain, she could manage only a crawl.

Sage thought quickly. "Wait here. I'll take the babies down and come back up and help you."

First, she dropped Trey's pack down the ladder. Then, pulse thwacking in her throat, she carried one infant down and placed her on the driest spot she could find before doing the same with the other.

By the time she topped the ladder for Barbara, her legs were wobbly.

"I can't stand," Barbara said.

"I'll carry you."

"Sage…"

Sage cut her off. "Piggyback ride, just like when we were kids. Hold on to me as tight as you can." Stuffing the flashlight into her pocket, she offered Barbara her back and Barbara cinched her arms tightly around Sage's shoulders. Painstakingly, using reserves of strength she didn't know she possessed, Sage got them to the bottom where they both collapsed in a heap, breathing hard.

Tears coursed over Barbara's face as she surveyed the dank-smelling lake.

"Are you hurt?" Sage said, kneeling there next to her.

"No, I'm just realizing something."

"What?"

She turned stricken eyes on Sage. "You can't carry me out of here and the babies, too."

Sage hadn't allowed her mind to consider that fact. "I'll carry them and then come back and carry you. We'll keep alternating like that."

Barbara's voice was stronger now, certain. "You need to leave me."

"No way," Sage said.

Barbara clasped her hand so tightly Sage winced.

"You cannot save us all. The babies have to get out. If there's time, come back for me."

"Barbara, I can't." She realized even as she said it that she had no choice. She could not save all three lives. The precious newborns would not last much longer in the cold and darkness with the addition of smoke-poisoned air. Pain lanced across her heart. "Trey might be back anytime," she whispered brokenly.

Barbara nodded and crawled over to the babies, who wriggled in their makeshift blankets. She kissed them tenderly and whispered to them. "Mommy loves you. Always remember that." Then she turned her face away. "Go now. Please, Sage."

Fighting tears, Sage pressed a bottle of water into Barbara's grasp. She tried to get her to keep the flashlight, too, but Barbara wouldn't hear of it, so she picked up the babies, her eyes overflowing and grief surging through her so strongly she thought it would stop her heart. "I'll come back as soon as I can." She looked once more toward the tunnel where Trey had gone. *Where are you?*

And then she clutched the babies as tightly as she dared and ran.

Trey sloshed back through the water, fighting down the fear. The smoke was thicker now, which meant the fire had caught somewhere at the upper levels. He made it back to the lake in record time, shouting as he entered the chamber.

"Sage?"

There was no answer. His worst nightmare. "Sage!" he thundered again, and this time there was a reply, a weak one, from the foot of the ladder to the catwalk. He found Barbara quickly. "What happened?"

"She couldn't carry us all so I told her to take the children. She found an exit at the rear."

"How long ago?"

"Just a few minutes."

"Perfect. All right. Let's go."

"You can't carry me," Barbara said, eyes round.

"Please, ma'am. You're talking to a guy who's used to a rucksack and forty-pound body armor. You're a feather." He got what he'd aimed for—a ghost of a smile from Barbara.

"You'll make someone a good husband," she said.

God willing. He lifted her as gently as he could manage, and though it would have been far easier to drape her over his shoulder, he carried her in his arms, her hands encircling his neck. The smoke smelled strong, and she turned her face toward his chest to avoid the fumes.

He found the exit quickly, grateful that it allowed him enough headroom to stand. The air smelled cleaner than in the chamber, and the floor was mercifully dry, seeming to slope upward from the underground chamber.

Forced to move slowly since he had no light to reveal any stumbling points, he pressed on.

Barbara spoke in his ear. "Sage thinks Derick is the one who locked me in the basement."

Trey was unsure how to respond, so he didn't.

She pressed. "I just want you to know it wasn't him, it was Fred Tipley. He probably did it for ransom."

"Oh," he managed to say.

"Fred will come clean when we find him."

He kept silent, focusing on putting one foot in front of the other without stumbling.

"What aren't you telling me?" Barbara pressed.

"This isn't the time to work through the details. Let's just get you out of here, okay?"

She squirmed in his arms. "You're keeping something back from me. I want to know right now."

He sighed. Determined women certainly did populate the family tree. She wanted the bare facts, and he'd give them to her. No sugarcoating. "We found Fred Tipley dead. He was shot."

Barbara went still in his arms. She sucked in several breaths before she answered. "It wasn't Derick," she whispered. "It wasn't."

Sage couldn't have much of a lead on them with babies to manage. The tunnel split into two. He stopped and listened, trying to detect any clue about which route she'd taken until his eyes fell on a saltwater taffy lying on the floor. About three yards ahead was another. He followed the candy trail Sage had left, smiling to himself.

"I heard a cry," Barbara said. They stopped to listen.

Trey had heard it, too. "Picking up the pace. Hold on."

He was almost jogging now, knowing the jolting was painful to her and half fearing it might cause her to bleed if there had been damage from the delivery. The baby's cry was shrill now, followed by a second wail.

"We're close," she breathed.

The tunnel widened and a flicker of light danced out of view a few yards ahead.

"Sage," he called out, panting with the effort. "Wait up."

He came to a stop after another yard. Sage stood in the middle of the tunnel, a baby in each arm. She stood stiffly, and as they drew closer he saw her jaw was clamped shut, lips thinned…in pain? In fear?

"What's wrong?" he said.

Another figure stepped from the shadows. "I think she's not very happy to see me," Rosalind said, the gun in her hand trained steadily on Sage and the babies.

TWENTY

Sage rocked the babies mechanically, her vision shifting from Rosalind to Trey and Barbara. Slowly, Trey released Barbara, who leaned shakily against the wall.

"Rosalind?" Barbara gasped. "What in the world are you doing?"

Rosalind shone the light on Barbara's face, forcing her to raise a hand to shield her eyes. "Barbara, even though you are nothing but trouble, I see you've managed to have the babies." Her face shone eagerly. "Boys or girls or both? Hopefully they favor Derick. Doesn't matter. We'll be happy with any combination."

Sage tried to warn Barbara to be quiet with a stern look that had no effect.

"We? Why would you say such a thing?" Barbara said. "Have you lost your senses?"

"No, Derick lost his senses when he married you."

Barbara jerked as if she'd been slapped.

"Rosalind was the one who had Fred lock you down here," Sage said.

"And I had him try to scare you two out of the opera house by sending the boxes down on you, but he was unable to complete the job as usual."

"Why did you have him lock me up?" Barbara's tone was incredulous.

"Because you're bankrupting Derick trying to restore this dump." She waved the flashlight around. "The poor man even thought of burning the place down rather than face disappointing you by revealing he's going broke."

"Broke? I had no idea."

"Of course you didn't," Rosalind spat. "Because you don't know him like I do. I've worked right alongside him since he was a nobody when he was struggling to get catalog shoots and he worked in my father's pizza shop. We've shared everything."

"Not everything," Trey said. "He didn't want to marry you, did he?"

Rosalind's eyes flashed. "He's always had his head turned by a pretty face and usually he winds up marrying them, or just making a fool of himself over the young ones, like he did with Antonia."

Barbara gaped.

"Oh, don't worry, honey, he never slept with her, just tried his macho caveman act, but she put him in his place."

Anger rippled across Barbara's face. "Don't talk to me about my husband."

"Not to worry, soon your name will be erased from our lives. I will make sure Derick knows you abandoned your twins and ran away with your secret lover. I am going to be an excellent mother to them. I've always known I would be the perfect woman to raise Derick's children."

Sage held the babies a little tighter. "That's why you locked her up in the first place. You meant to murder her after the babies were born and take them."

"Someone had to save Derick from being ruined by this woman." Rosalind shrugged. "Good plan, except the earthquake was unexpected. Fred panicked and insisted on getting little Miss Barbara out of the basement."

"So you killed him."

"So I did." She sniffed.

"And you set the fire, too?" Trey said.

"Enough talking."

"Tell us," Sage said, "or I'm not handing over these babies."

"I think you will. I've worked too hard for them." She coughed. "I've inhaled more toxic smoke than a person should."

Sage felt sickened. "You set the gasoline cans on fire to kill us, and Barbara, too."

"Seemed like as good a solution as any, but just

in case, I came back to make sure all the loose ends were tied up. So good of you to deliver the kiddos. Are they both healthy? If not, I'll be happy with one. Could be you decided to keep one when you ran away with Mr. Right." She moved closer and Sage snatched the infants out of reach, backing toward Trey and Barbara.

"Stay away from my children," Barbara hissed.

"They should be my children," Rosalind said through gritted teeth. "They're going to be my babies and he's my man, and you three are going to die here, right now, and no one will be the wiser." She flicked the gun at Sage. "Put them down and walk away."

Sage forced out an answer. "I won't do it."

Rosalind's lip curled. "Yes, you will." She aimed the gun at Barbara. "I can kill her quickly or you can watch her suffer. Have you got the stomach for that?"

Sage's gut twisted in horror. What could she do? She looked helplessly at Trey, noticing his slight movement. He was going to attack, to throw himself on Rosalind and give them a chance to escape.

No, she mouthed, agony lancing through her.

Trey's eyes were calm. *Yes,* they seemed to say.

She spun to face Rosalind, her body in front of Trey. *Please let me find a way out of this.*

"Derick won't believe Barbara just abandoned her children."

"Hmm. He believed she's been in Santa Fe all this time. The occasional text from Barbara's phone was enough to convince him. Derick is many things, but he's not whip-smart, I'm afraid. He won't ask too many questions."

"People will be looking for Barbara."

"What people?" She wiggled the gun back and forth. "Her parents are dead and her devoted cousin?" Rosalind said and then laughed. "Must have died in the opera house fire or, if there's enough of your body left to find the bullet hole, maybe she was killed by the same looters that shot Fred Tipley."

"Rosalind, what happened to make you like this?" Barbara said.

Rosalind's face pinched. "Just got tired of watching everyone else get what I should have had. Enough talk now," she barked at Sage. "Put the babies down. Gently. I don't want them damaged."

"How are you going to hide them until you sell Derick on your story that Barbara abandoned them?"

She shrugged. "I'll figure something out. Quit stalling."

Sage knelt and eased the babies onto the ground. She fought hard not to cry, eyes scanning the ground for something, anything she could use as a weapon. She found nothing. Trey put a hand on her shoulder to keep her kneeling there.

No, no, her mind shouted in a silent entreaty. *Don't sacrifice yourself.*

"Wait," she yelled, whirling toward Rosalind. "I have to give them water."

"Water? Babies drink milk."

"Barbara is dehydrated. She doesn't have enough. If I don't get them some water, they might die before you get out of here with them."

Rosalind shifted. "Fine. Give them water."

"Okay." With shaking hands, Sage rooted around in the pack, her back to Rosalind. Blocking Rosalind's view with her body, she handed Trey the hammer. He took it and before she could rise, he hurled the hammer as hard as he could. It slammed into Rosalind's shoulder and she staggered back. Trey leapt forward and Rosalind fired twice. The first bullet ricocheted off the stone walls. Barbara screamed and Sage caged her body over the babies to protect them.

The second bullet pinged off the stone and buried itself into the floor by Sage's feet. She looked over her shoulder and saw Trey two feet from Rosalind, who had recovered enough to wield the gun at his chest.

"You're not going to kill them," he panted.

"I'll shoot you down right now."

"Then do it," he commanded. "But you better get the shot perfect because I'm coming for you."

Sage screamed when Rosalind's finger tightened

on the trigger just as a rock sailed through the air and smacked into the ceiling. Rosalind looked up and Trey took that split second to bring her to the floor, wrenching the gun away and turning her facedown, his knee between her shoulders.

Sage was too terrified to make sense of what had happened until Dallas ran in, breathing hard.

"Was that you that threw the rock?" Trey said.

"Yeah." His eyes scanned the room. "Everyone okay?"

Trey nodded. "Would have been better if you'd hit her."

Dallas grinned. "You always told me I couldn't hit the broad side of a barn."

Sage found herself laughing, though it sounded half-hysterical. "Why did you come back?"

"I found an old guy trying to get his cat out of a buried car so I stuck around to help him. Took all night to dig that tabby out and then one thing led to another," he said. "As I was getting ready to split, I noticed this gal entering one of the drain pipes." He gestured to Rosalind. "I figured it bore some checking out. Besides," he said with a grin, "I forgot my hat."

Sage threw Trey a short rope from the duffel bag and he secured Rosalind's hands behind her back before he hauled her to her feet.

She aimed a poisonous look at Barbara. "I deserved him. You never did."

Barbara lifted her chin. "I'll make sure to tell him all about you, Rosalind. Believe me, you're going to get exactly what you deserve."

Trey handed her over to Dallas, who swept an arm gallantly toward the direction from which he had emerged. "Right this way," he said.

Trey helped Sage to her feet and she wrapped her arms around him, unable to speak. Finally, when her breath returned enough, she whispered in his ear, "I was so scared."

He stroked her back and she was comforted by the rapid thud of his heartbeat. "But you didn't give up. You fought back, right up to the end and we won. Mission accomplished."

One of the babies began to cry and Sage felt like doing the same, but she forced a smile. "Not mission accomplished until we get Barbara and her babies out of here."

"Copy that," he said. He put on his pack and walked to Barbara, and once again lifted her gingerly while Sage gathered up the babies, snuggling them close to try and warm them.

After one final glance around the decrepit underbelly of the Imperial, she headed out, her arms filled with two precious bundles.

The police arrived the next morning at the overburdened San Francisco Memorial Hospital. Trey had spent a few hours prowling the hallways, pacing until he heard the news that Barbara was okay, and wondering where Sage had gotten to.

Finally, he was allowed to go see Barbara. Her face had more color, but she was thin and wan, scratches etching her face and a dark bruise under one eye. After a battery of tests, the doctors determined she was suffering from an infection and a badly sprained ankle. Not surprising, Trey thought, considering. He stayed with her awhile, letting her talk, filling in the details when he could, but all the while wondering where Sage was.

"The babies are doing well," Barbara said, as if reading his mind, "and Sage promised she would stick close by their bassinets in the nursery. She's hardly left their sides, from what I've been told."

"That sounds like her."

Barbara raised an eyebrow. "She's devoted to people she loves. I think you both share that trait."

He wasn't sure how to respond. Every time he thought about Sage something burned inside him, something warm and wonderful that made him start pacing again. He did so now, wandering around the small room, to the window, back to the door.

Barbara gave him a smile. "I can't ever thank you both enough. You saved me and my babies."

"It was Sage. To be honest, it seemed too far-fetched to believe you were really trapped down there. I was pretty sure you were in New Mexico."

She laughed. "But you went in anyway, to save us."

To save Sage. It was the truth, he couldn't deny it even to himself.

She yawned widely. "Would it be all right if I took a little rest now? I'm sure Sage wouldn't mind if you checked in on her."

Feeling as if Barbara was not nearly as tired as she appeared, he headed to the nursery and peered through the glass windows. He watched Sage, wearing clean clothes borrowed from the hospital that dwarfed her small frame, rocking the babies one at a time.

She smiled occasionally at some small gesture or expression from the little ones and her face was so filled with peace, so unbelievably beautiful.

Derick joined him at the window, staring at his two children, incredulous.

"I just can't believe it. Rosalind was going to kill Barbara and Sage and take the children." His voice shook. "I was an idiot not to see through her, but it was always so much easier to let Rosalind handle everything rather than question it." His head dropped. "I abdicated my role as husband. Barbara will never forgive me for planning to torch the Imperial or letting Rosalind take her, or for making a fool of myself with Antonia." His lip trembled and he was no longer the youthful screen star, but a tired, washed-up actor, tortured by regret.

Trey felt a mixture of pity and disgust, but pity won out. He clapped a hand on Derick's shoulder. "You've both got two really important reasons to get past this."

Derick's brow wrinkled and then he looked through the nursery glass. "Two important reasons," he echoed.

"You bet. So why don't you get started by seeing if there's anything you can do for your wife? She's been through a lot more than you have. Time to man up."

Derick smiled and looked like he was going to lay a hug on Trey, so he stepped back a safe distance.

"Thanks."

"Anytime," Trey said.

Alone again in the hallway, he returned to watching Sage soothe the little girl whom he'd been told was to be called Elizabeth Sage. His heart seemed to swell inside him at the delicacy and strength that showed itself in her. Those graceful hands that now embraced the most fragile life had carried the infants through fire and bullets to safety.

She was not the same woman he had discovered in the theater before the big quake. And he was not the same man.

When she finally put the babies down and took

off the nursery smock, he held the door for her as she stepped into the hallway.

"Morning," he said.

"Good morning. You don't have Wally with you. I'm surprised."

"No canine visitors allowed. Emiliano is keeping him until I pick him up this afternoon."

"Before you go." She looked away. "I thought you would already be gone to that place you're building in the mountains."

"Not until I made sure everyone was properly accounted for."

She smiled. "Completed your mission. Well, Captain Black, I can tell you that Sage Harrington has returned from the front."

He caught something under her teasing tone. "Is that right?"

"Yes, that's right." She sighed. "I've been wandering around in guilt and fear, but I think I'm ready to get well now. Seeing those little babies come into the world kind of reminded me how much joy God has in store for me."

His heart beat quicker. "That is excellent news."

"And," she said quietly, "I'm going to get help, if I need it, to get completely well again."

"Sage, I'm proud of you."

She stood on tiptoe and kissed him on the cheek. "Thank you for helping me get to that place."

His cheek warmed at her touch, painting trails

of happiness through his body. "My pleasure," he said, "but you got there mostly by yourself."

She looked away again. "Anyway, I just wanted to make sure I said that, before you left."

At that moment, something that had been shadowed shone clear as a diamond in his soul. *Go ahead, Black.* Without the slightest hesitation, he reached for her hand. "What if I didn't?"

"Didn't what?"

His nerves jangled and the words tumbled out, tangling up in each other. "What if I didn't leave? What if I stayed here, or anywhere, where you are?" He was blabbering like a teenage boy.

"Why would you do that?" She fixed those sapphire eyes on him, the color so vibrant it almost hurt. Was there anything as beautiful as that gaze, which had so many dark moments and hardwon triumphs embedded deep down? Was there a woman as perfectly courageous and willing to fight her way, with God's help, through unbelievable horrors to save her cousin and herself? The answer was no, and Trey was not about to let Sage Harrington get away again.

He drew himself up to full height, back stiff, army-strong. "Let me just say this in the easiest way. Ma'am, I am one hundred percent nuts about you."

She gasped, mouth falling open. "What?"

He forged ahead, in crisp commanding tones.

"In spite of your flagrant disregard for proper military conduct, I am unable to imagine my life without you."

Her expression was caught halfway between wonder and disbelief. "What are you saying?"

"Miss Sage Harrington, I believe it is my duty and pleasure to pursue you until you are convinced of the value of my mission."

Her face split into a brilliant grin. "Did you bump your head back there in the tunnel?"

"Ma'am, no, ma'am. It's all about the mission, as stated."

"What exactly would that mission be?"

He stood ramrod-straight. "That you would consent to be my joint commander, wife and partner, ma'am."

Now she was laughing, a rich, throaty laugh that thrilled him to the core. "Captain Black, are you sure you want to pursue this mission in light of the fact that your joint commander is prone to disobey orders and go AWOL?"

"Ma'am, yes, ma'am." He reached for her now, joy shuddering through him as if the very ground beneath his feet was shaking. In a low throaty voice, he spoke into her ear, "I love you. All we've been through has shown both of us at our best and worst. I know exactly who you are and I want you by my side forever." He did not let her wiggle out of his arms. "What say you, Sage Harrington? Will you join in my mission?"

She circled his neck with her arms and lifted her mouth to his. "I say that's an affirmative, Captain Black."

He allowed the shock wave to travel through his muscles and fibers. Sage Harrington was his, now and forever. Delight tightened his belly, the kiss shaking the truth into him. At long last, out of the darkest disaster and the horror of war, had come the sweet taste of rejoicing. They were both finally home.

* * * * *

Dear Reader,

Here in California we are used to occasional earthquakes and most of the time they pass by unnoticed. We are warned to prepare for the "big one," that massive earthquake that forecasters tell us is coming. I remember chatting with my mother in 1989 when the Loma Prieta quake hit during the World Series between the San Francisco Giants and the Oakland A's. Measuring 6.9 on the Richter scale, it lasted only 15 to 20 seconds, but what an impact those seconds made. The quake killed 62 people, caused billions of dollars in property damage and resulted in 22 structural fires and the collapse of buildings and a span of the Bay Bridge.

My mother and I ran into the front yard and saw the street rolling and pitching like waves on the ocean. I remember thinking how much power I was witnessing at that very moment, and how powerless I was in the face of such a massive display.

We know that God is mighty, a world maker and a destroyer at times. Yet His incredible power is balanced by the care and attention He gives to His people, weak and fragile though we are. I hope you enjoy this story about two people discovering that their strength and ability to survive life's disasters comes from the Lord. Yes, the whole earth may quake, but we are still cradled in the palm of One who loves us without measure.

One of my greatest joys is hearing from my readers. If you would like to send a comment, or share your thoughts, please do feel free to contact me via my website at www.danamentink.com. If you prefer to communicate via the written word, there is a physical address there as well.

God bless,

Dana Mentink

Questions for Discussion

1. Have you ever experienced an earthquake or other natural disaster? Share about your experience.

2. Sage suffers from post-traumatic stress disorder (PTSD), as do many of our soldiers returning from Iraq and Afghanistan. How best can we support these struggling men and women on a personal level?

3. Sage and Trey come from different worlds. How are their viewpoints similar? How are they different?

4. Trey doesn't carry a cell phone because he feels they are intrusive. Do you share his feelings? Why or why not?

5. Sage is terrified to show her weakness to Trey. What things do we do to hide our weaknesses from others?

6. Sage feels defeated by her choices and the world around her. What is the Biblical antidote for this feeling?

7. Disasters bring out the best and worst in people. Do you agree or disagree? Why?

8. Sage believes that everyone fights on their own personal battlefield. Describe a battle you have fought. How has God helped you struggle through it?

9. Our society relies heavily on cell phones and the internet. What problems would you expect if both were rendered useless by a disaster?

10. Why is forgiveness so hard to extend and sometimes just as hard to accept?

11. What are your impressions of Dallas Black, Trey's brother?

12. Staying trapped in regret and guilt is paralyzing. What advice does the Bible have for moving beyond such a situation?

13. Is it possible to forgive, but not forget? Explain.

14. Have you had a time in your life when you felt lost? How did God help you through?

15. What challenges will the city of San Francisco face in the aftermath of the earthquake? Are there Biblical examples of how God helps his people rebuild?

LARGER-PRINT BOOKS!

GET 2 FREE
LARGER-PRINT NOVELS
PLUS 2 FREE
MYSTERY GIFTS

Love Inspired

SUSPENSE
RIVETING INSPIRATIONAL ROMANCE

Larger-print novels are now available...

ReaderService.com

Manage your account online!

- Review your order history
- Manage your payments
- Update your address

*We've designed
the Harlequin® Reader Service
website just for you.*

Enjoy all the features!

- Reader excerpts from any series
- Respond to mailings and special monthly offers
- Discover new series available to you
- Browse the Bonus Bucks catalog
- Share your feedback

Visit us at:

ReaderService.com

RS13